S0-BAA-850

Anointed Inspirations Publishing

Presents

The Pastor's Lie

By

Shanika Roach

ALL RIGHTS RESERVED. No part of this publication may be reproduced, distributed or transmitted in any form or by any means, including photocopying, recording, or other electronic or mechanical methods, without the prior written permission of the publisher, except in the case of brief quotations embodied in critical reviews and certain other noncommercial uses permitted by copyright law. For more information, please contact the publisher.

Copyright © 2018 Shanika Roach
Published by Anointed Inspirations Publishing, LLC

Note: This is a work of fiction. Names, characters, places and incidents either are products of the author's imagination or are used fictitiously. Any resemblance to actual events or locales or persons, living or dead, is entirely coincidental

Anointed Inspirations Publishing is currently accepting Urban Christian Fiction, Inspirational Romance, and Young Adult fiction submissions. For consideration, please send manuscripts to anointedinspirationspublishing@gmail.com

CHAPTER 1

Michelle

I gripped the phone tightly in my hand as I listened to my mother in disbelief.

"He doesn't have too much time left. The doctor gave him a couple of weeks left to live." My mother said.

I squeezed my eyes shut to prevent the tears from falling, but I lost the battle and they fell anyway. My father was diagnosed with stage four pancreatic cancer six months ago, and it was devastating to our family. "I just saw dad two months ago, and the doctors were hopeful that he would have at least a few more months." I choked out through tears.

"I know, but he's rapidly declining." My mother paused as if she was hesitating to tell me something else."

"What is it mom?" I asked.

"Well, your father wants you to take over his church. He told me before I left his hospital room about twenty minutes ago." My mom confessed.

"What? I can't do that. I have my own church to lead." I said as I wiped my tears away with the back of my hand.

"I know but this is something he really wants you to do."

I took a deep breath. This was a lot to take in. "I thought he would leave the church to his assistant pastor, Dan."

"Your father wants to leave his church to family, and well your brother…" my mom said and then she stopped talking.

There was no need for her to say anything else. My brother Jeff was in no way ready to take on the responsibility of leading the church, but I knew he was probably giving my father a fit about that. That's all he talked about when I visited a few months ago. "I understand dad wants me to lead his church, but I have to really think about this. I'll be in Kansas City by this weekend."

"Okay, good. I'll see you then dear." My mom said, and we ended the call.

I sat my cell phone down on coffee table and tried to gather myself. My mother just laid a lot on me. Not only would my father probably be dead in a couple of weeks, but he wanted me to take over his church, and honestly, I didn't know if that was even possible. I was a Pastor at my own church Faith and Love Christian Center. The path to having my own church was a rocky ride. I was born and raised in Kansas City, Missouri. Growing up I always had a passion to learn everything about the bible. I went to church every Sunday and I also attended bible study, but I would naturally be there because my father Louis Davis is the head Pastor of his church God's Kingdom Worship Center. He started out with a very small church and it grew over the years and now it was one of the largest churches in Missouri. My mother Evelyn is the assistant superintendent of schools, so her job was busy, but she was an excellent first lady and mother to me and my brother Jeffrey. When I went to school I was known as the preacher's kid, so my classmates would always ask me questions about the bible, and even try to contradict some of the things in the bible. They said that some of the stuff didn't make sense, and I would try to answer their questions the best way I could, and what I couldn't answer I would ask my father about it, and he explained to me that people would always have questions about the bible and sometimes no matter how much you try to explain things to them they would still come to their own conclusions. After continuously becoming frustrated with my classmates' questions, it didn't take me long to figure out he was right about this. But it bothered me so much because I really wanted people to have a clear understanding of the bible, so after I graduated from high school, I went to college in Memphis, Tennessee and majored in theology. That's when I met my now ex-husband Jason Roberts, during my freshman year. Jason was a sophomore majoring in computer science. He was so handsome and charming, and he swept me off my feet. He was such a good singer. The first time I heard him sing I knew I was in love. I used to love it when he sung Forever My Lady by Jodeci to me. I didn't date much in high school because I was focused on my studies, and I was also still a virgin at the time because I tried to always live by God's word. Jason is light-skinned with a nice lean build and he is about 6'0 tall. I have a smooth peanut butter complexion and shoulder length hair. I am 5'7 and I'm a size eight. We were a striking looking couple, and people often told us that on campus. After graduating from college Jason and I got married. Jason could sing so well that he got a record contract to sing gospel music. I was so happy for him, and then I went on to get my master's degree, but then I got pregnant with our daughter Courtney in the middle of graduate school. We were very happy to be having a child, but it was a lot for us to deal with because Jason's career was taking off at the time, so he wasn't home as much to help me. I took a year off after Courtney was born, and then I went on to finish graduate school with the help from a nanny. My plan was to teach theology class at a college, but I felt I had a different calling. God was calling me to preach and at first, I tried to ignore it, but I couldn't and when I told Jason he was very supportive of me. I learned so much from my father, so it wasn't hard for me to start my own church. It started off small, but it grew over the years and now I had about ten thousand members at my church, and I was asked to preach all over the country, but all this came with a price.

Jason and I were very passionate about our careers. Jason thought I should step back a little, so I could have more time for Courtney and him, and I thought he should do the same. I was a Pastor of my church and he should have made more of an effort to be by my side. Then there were rumors that he was having an affair with Leslie Tom one of his label mates, but of course he denied it, and I had no other choice but to believe him because I didn't have proof. I tried to make it work, but I couldn't ignore my calling and join him on the road and be at every awards show with him. I wasn't some arm piece trophy wife, and he didn't just want to be a first man who follows his wife around. We tried, and we tried but neither of us were willing to budge, and finally we both decided to throw in the towel. The fights and the silent treatment were too much to deal with. It was hard because I was a Pastor. I had failed at my marriage. My congregation was surprised but understanding. The divorce was very painful, and to further aggravate my pain Jason and Leslie began dating shortly after and were married about a year later. Watching them perform together and give interviews together felt like someone stabbed me in the stomach with a knife and kept twisting it. I yelled at Jason and demanded to know if something had been going on with him and Leslie the whole time and he admitted to me that he had developed feelings for Leslie and they had shared a kiss, but that was as far as it went until we were divorced. It hurt me to hear that, but I was glad that he had told me. It was a rough period in my life. My daughter blamed me for the divorce. She was such a daddy's girl. I could relate because I was a daddy's girl too. It was a difficult time, but I managed to get through it. I'm forty-one now, and I gained wisdom from all of it.

Thinking of all this reminded me how upset Courtney would be if I decided to move back to Kansas City. She loved Memphis and I knew she didn't want to leave her friends. She was now sixteen. This was all too much. I closed my eyes and prayed to God for direction.

CHAPTER 2

Jeffrey

The moment my mother left my father's hospital room, I let my father know how upset I was about his decision. It took everything in me to remain silent as my father told my mother that he was appointing my sister the new pastor. I was so angry I was surprised steam wasn't coming out of my ears. "So, you're really going to let Michelle run the church?" I asked bitterly. I stared intently at my father. He was so gaunt, but he was very much lucid.

"Jeff, you know you're not ready to lead the church." My father said weakly.

"But I'm your oldest child, your only son."

"I'm aware of that, but Michelle is better suited to run the church and you know it." my father said not backing down.

"She has her own church that she has to worry about and plus she is a single Pastor and divorced at that." I pointed out. I was going to throw everything out there to plead my case, and I didn't care about throwing my sister under the bus in the process.

My father gave me a sympathetic look. "I don't like how you try to find fault with your sister especially when you have things going on in your life that aren't so great."

I looked at my father in shock. Just what was he implying here. *He couldn't possibly know about that, or could he?"* "What are you trying to say, Dad?"

My father closed his eyes for a moment and then reopened them, and I knew he was getting tired. "It doesn't matter son because my mind is made up, Michelle will be leading the church."

His words caused my body to feel hot and I felt like a volcano about to erupt. "You always treated her like she was a princess like she could do no wrong but mark my words you will not be able to rest peacefully in the afterlife because Michelle is not perfect, and she will probably bring the church down!" I yelled.

A nurse entered the room. "What's going on in here?" she asked as she looked at me suspiciously.

"We were just talking." I said suddenly feeling guilty. Here my father was lying on his soon to be death bed and I was arguing with him.

The nurse started to say something else but was interrupted when my father started gasping for air. I turned around to look at him as the nurse rushed to assist him. The monitors started beeping loudly.

"What's the matter, is he alright?" I asked frantically

"I'm sorry you have to leave." The nurse said.

I slowly backed out of the room while a few doctors rushed in the room to assist my father. I nervously sat in the waiting area. I wasn't a monster. I love my father and care about his health, but I wanted to run the church, and it was a conversation that needed to be had no matter the circumstances. I believed as his son that I earned that right. Twenty minutes later two doctors walked over to me with grim looks on their faces and I knew what the news would be.

"I'm so sorry we did everything we could, but your father's heart failed, and we were unable to resuscitate him." One of the doctors said.

It felt as if someone snatched my heart out of my chest. "I don't understand, I was just talking to him." I said weakly.

The doctor gave me a sympathetic look. "I know, your father's heart and his other organs were weak from the cancer. We're sorry for your loss."

The doctors were still talking, but I didn't hear anything else they were saying. Was this my fault? Did my words kill my father? Those thoughts were so unbearable that I had to get out of the hospital immediately. I hurried out of the hospital and almost knocked over a few people in the process. I ignored their shouts as I hurried to my Audi A4. Once inside my car, I sat there for a moment trying to gather myself. Tears started pouring down my face. I couldn't believe the great Louis Davis was gone from this earth.

Growing up I always respected and wanted to be like my father, but I could never live up to his expectations, but my sister did. She was good, and it came natural for her. I struggled, I got in trouble in school a lot even though we went to school at a private Christian academy. My grades were terrible, and I also shoplifted. I don't know why I did it, stealing gave me a rush. Even when I got caught and my father gave me a stern warning I still did it. I was lucky that I didn't get arrested because the owner of the store respected and admired my father, so he didn't press charges. I continued to shoplift. I just took extra precautions, so I wouldn't get caught. I changed a little when I met a beautiful sweet Christian girl named Valerie who would later become my wife.

She was beautiful with her olive completion and wavy hair thanks to her mixed heritage. Her mother was German, and her father was black. She had a nice petite figure and she stood at about 5'4 inches. I'm brown skinned with a bald head and I'm 5'll. Most women considered me handsome, and I keep my body in shape. Valerie was very smart and that made me want to get my act together and I started studying a lot and my grades were good enough for me to get into college. Valerie and I went to different colleges, but we still made time to see each other on the weekend. Valerie majored in accounting and I wanted to impress her and my father, so I majored in science. That was a big mistake because it was too hard for me and I eventually flunked out of college. Valerie told me it was okay, and that she still loved me. I believed that she loved me, but it was embarrassing, and it didn't help matters that my little sister was majoring in theology and doing well.

After flunking out of college, I came back home to live, but my father told me if I wasn't going to college than I had to get a job. My father talked to one of his friends who owned a mechanic shop and asked him if he needed any help. He hired me, but working in mechanics was not my thing. I didn't like some of the rude people that came in the shop complaining about the prices. I started coming into work late. I mean I was already depressed that I flunked out of college while my woman was in school close to getting her degree. My father's friend talked to me about being late and so did my father, but I continued to be late and I half did my job at the shop, so his friend had no other choice but to fire me. I didn't care, but my father was furious at me and concerned about my future. That's when my mother stepped in and she talked to me about going back to college even if it was community college, but I wasn't interested in going back to college. I eventually got a job at the supermarket. The pay was alright. Valerie told me she was happy that I found a job that I liked. Her words were comforting, but what she didn't know was that I start messing around with different girls. I loved Valerie, but the other attention from women made me feel good.

After graduating from college, Valerie got her master's degree, and found a nice townhouse. I had gotten raises at the supermarket, and I eventually moved out of parent's house and found me a one-bedroom apartment. I proposed to Valerie, and we married a year later, and I moved into her townhouse. It made me feel less than a man that my wife was making more money than me, and I had moved into her home. I talked to my father about it, and he let me work as a deacon at his church. He told me that I had to be a sincere Christian man, or he would let me go as a deacon. I assured him that I would be the best deacon that I could be. My father took me at my word, and he paid me a nice salary, but by then Valerie was working as a Chartered Financial Analyst for an investment company, and she was making a nice six figure salary. We moved into a nice four-bedroom two-story house. We had two sons Omar and Daniel.

Our life was nice and comfortable, but when things are going well, there is always a storm that can come through at any time. My wife's older sister Ingrid died in a house fire leaving her daughter behind and being the caring woman that she is my wife let her niece Naomi who was seventeen at the time move in with us. Naomi almost died from smoke inhalation, but she recovered from her injuries. Naomi is beautiful just like my wife, she could basically pass as her daughter. Naomi got along well with my sons and I tried to be a father figure for her because Naomi never knew her father. Whenever I did things with my boys, I included her as well. She was depressed a lot, but she eventually started coming around. But somewhere along the way, Naomi started looking at me with interest. I tried to ignore the longing looks she gave me and the flirting. I kept reminding myself that her interest in me was misplaced. She was missing her mother, and she was mistaking my kindness for something else. But it felt good to get attention from a young beautiful woman. She looked at me as no woman ever looked at me before. It was good for my ego since I felt drowned by my wife's success. Sure, other women were attracted to me, but Naomi looked at me like I was her hero, and with so much admiration in her eyes, and I gave in to temptation. The first time was when she stayed home from school because she said she was sick, and we were left alone together, but I would later find out that was an excuse for her to make her move on me. After that one time, we kept sneaking around together, and my wife had no idea. I was quite certain that nothing like that had ever entered her mind because she had total trust in me. But my luck ran out when my oldest son Omar caught us kissing. He was furious with me, but I managed to calm him down and told him it was just that one kiss and that it would never happen again. He said he wouldn't tell his mother because he didn't want to see the hurt look on her face, and that if it was just one kiss and wouldn't happen again then it was no need to upset her. My son kept my secret, but he became cold and distant from me.

Naomi became pregnant a year after our affair, and she gave birth to my son Desmond. Fortunately, Desmond looked just like her. Omar was suspicious at first, but Naomi told everyone the father of her baby was this guy she hooked up with a few times and that he didn't want to have anything to do with her or the baby. Everyone bought the story, and my wife adored Desmond. Desmond only knew me as his uncle because I couldn't let on that

I was his father. Omar, who is now nineteen went away to college in Springfield. He is majoring in software engineering. He is smart just like my wife.

I helped Naomi move out of our house and into a decent two-bedroom apartment. I helped her with the rent, and she has a job working at a daycare and Desmond also goes to the daycare, so it's very convenient for her. Desmond is now three years old, and my secret is still safe. My father's words led me to believe that he possibly knew that Desmond was my son, but how could he know? He never let on that he knew anything. I guess it didn't matter now, but I hoped he didn't tell my mother and most of all I hoped he didn't tell my big shot sister. I'm forty-three years old now, and I held a lot of envy and resentment towards Michelle. At my age I should know better, but I couldn't help the way that I felt. She went on the have her own church just like my father. Everyone was impressed that a father and daughter achieved so much. It did make me feel good when her marriage imploded for all the world to see. It should have been me who achieved that. I would have loved to be known all over the world for my great preaching skills and bringing people to Christ, but I knew I wasn't the good person my sister was. It doesn't matter how good a person is, no one is perfect, and I wanted to see my sister fall flat on her face.

CHAPTER 3

Michelle

After praying, I decided I would move back to Kansas City. I would keep my house here in Memphis. I would leave my church in the capable hands of my assistant pastor Deon. I could still come to Memphis a couple times a month to check in on my house and church. I couldn't give up my house that I loved so much. Jason and I had it designed ourselves. It is a beautiful mansion with five bedrooms. I know I would miss my bedroom that had a nice fireplace in it. I would buy a condo or townhouse in Kansas City. I had been looking online at apartments. Even though my mind was made up, I was still nervous because I had to tell Courtney.

I had cooked a nice dinner of shrimp pasta, a fruit salad, and rolls. Courtney loved shrimp pasta. I was trying to soften the blow. I was waiting for her to get home from school. She had to stay late to take a make-up test that she missed last week because she was sick.

I was setting the table when Courtney walked in. "It smells good in here." Courtney said smiling. My daughter was beautiful. She had her father's light-skinned, and she looked like both of us.

"Yes, I made your favorite."

"Good, because I can't wait to eat. That physics test was hard, but I think I made at least a B." Courtney said as she helped me set the table.

After the table was set, and our plates fixed, we sat down to eat. "So is this a special occasion because you don't cook that much." Courtney pointed out.

I couldn't help but smile. My daughter was very smart. "Actually, there is something very important that I need to discuss with you."

Courtney raised her eyebrow and stopped eating. "What's going on?" she asked in a worried tone.

I took a sip of my raspberry tea and then said. "Your grandfather's condition has gotten worse, and he only has a couple of weeks to live now."

Courtney gasped. "Oh no."

I paused for a moment because I knew what I was about to say next was going to stun her. "My mother informed me that my father wants me to lead his church after he is gone."

A confused expression came across Courtney's face. "How are you going to do that when you lead your own church?"

"I would have to move back to Kansas City, and let my assistant pastor take over, but I would come back here at least twice a month."

"I don't want to move to Kansas City, I like it here. This is where I grew up."

"I know honey, but I have to do this for my father."

"Why can't he appoint someone else to lead the church." Courtney asked in an unhappy tone.

"Because he wants to leave the church with family."

Courtney shook her head. "Well I don't want to move to Kansas City." She said stubbornly.

"Too bad because we're moving." I was starting to get upset now. She wasn't going to tell me where she wasn't going to move.

"Okay, if I have to move than I rather move in with my father in LA."

My mouth dropped open in shock. I wasn't expecting her to say that at all, and it hurt that she would rather live with her father and stepmother than me. "What sense does it make to move out to LA with your father when you've been living with me all this time." I finally said after the shock had worn off.

"Because I would have more stability with them. You just said that you would be coming back here twice a month, so you probably won't have much time with me now anyway."

It was true that I would probably have less time with her, but she would still be my priority. I could see why she would think living with them would be more stable than me since Jason and Leslie's careers had slowed down some, but they still were busy people just like me. "I would make time for you of course, and plus you will be around family."

Courtney pouted, and I was about to make another point when the phone rang. I got up from the table and answered the phone in the kitchen.

"Michelle, your father is gone." My mother squeaked out with so much pain in her voice.

My body froze. "How can that be mom. You just told me he had a couple more weeks." I managed to get out.

"I know, but your brother just informed me that your father just died. Apparently, his heart just gave out."

I dropped the phone and slid to the floor and let out a cry. I wanted to talk to my father and spend time with him before he died, and now that wasn't going to be possible. Courtney ran over to me and sat beside me and wrapped her arms around me as I cried. I couldn't believe that the next time I saw my father he would be in a casket.

CHAPTER 4

Michelle

A week later, I sat on the first row of my father's funeral in a daze. This seemed so surreal. The church was packed. Pastor's from all over the world came to my father's funeral to pay their respect. I just sat there numbly as tears streamed down my face, staring at my father's casket. We had picked out a beautiful bronze casket for him. My father was sixty-five years old, and I felt that he still had a lot of more years left to live. It seemed unfair that he was stricken with cancer, but it was in God's will.

I managed to get through the funeral and the burial site, but I did break down when they lowered his casket in the ground, and now we were headed back to my mother's house. When we arrived at my mother's house, her house quickly began to fill with guests. I felt overwhelmed, but Courtney and I along with Valerie helped my mother out in the kitchen. My mother looked like she was about to break down a couple of times, but she held strong.

I was arranging the cakes on the counter when my best friend Regina Tyson walked into the kitchen with her son Bradley. I saw her briefly at the funeral, but it was so many people there that I didn't get a chance to talk to her. Regina was a pretty, medium brown-skinned woman with a voluptuous figure that men loved, and women envied. Regina was one of the first girls to get her figure in the sixth grade. Her hair was in neat spiral curls.

She walked over to us. She gave me a tight hug. "It's so good to see you, but I'm sorry that it had to be under these circumstances." She said as she hugged my mother next. "My mother told me to tell you she's sorry she couldn't make it because she isn't feeling well." She said to my mother.

"I understand." My mother responded.

"It's good to see you too." and I meant it. It would be nice to be around my best friend again on a permanent basis. She attended my father's church, well now my church. Then I looked at Bradley who had a shy look on his face. He was a tall handsome light brown boy with a lean frame. "Hello, there Bradley I haven't seen you in a while. You have grown to be such a handsome guy." I said and reached out to hug him.

"Thanks." He said with a smile.

I looked over to my daughter. She was staring at Bradley intently and he was looking at my daughter as well. "Bradley this is my daughter, Courtney." I introduced.

"Hey." Bradley said.

My daughter spoke back with a huge smile on her face and Regina looked at me with raised eyebrows. These two were obviously smitten with each other.

The moment was broken up when Valerie walked over to us. "You guys can go catch up and I'll help Ms. Evelyn in the kitchen."

"Oh no, I'm here to help. We can catch up and help at the same time." Regina said.

We got to work setting up the drinks and the food. While working my mother had a weary look on her face. "Mom why don't you go lie down, and we can finish up in here."

"No, it would be rude to go lie down while there are guests in the house." She said.

"Don't worry about the guests, they will understand."

"She's right." Valerie agreed.

My mother started to protest, but then she just nodded and left the kitchen. After we finished setting up the kitchen, we went out into the living room to entertain the guests. The huge living room were filled with people. I looked around and noticed my daughter talking to Bradley in the corner of the room. My nephews Omar and Daniel were sitting down on the couch watching TV. But I noticed one person that was missing and that was my brother. I wondered where he was.

When Valerie came out of the kitchen, I stopped her. "Where is Jeff?" I asked her.

"Oh, just before we left the burial site, he said one of his friends' car broke down and he went to go help him."

"Okay." I said, but something didn't seem right about that. I wasn't going to voice my skepticism to Valerie because she was blindly loyal to my brother.

And when an hour passed by and my brother still didn't show up, I became concerned. This was our father's repast after all. Just what was Jeff up to?

CHAPTER 5

Jeffrey

I just left the emergency room with Naomi and Desmond. Naomi had planned to go to the funeral, but Desmond became sick. She kept texting me at the funeral, and I ignored all of her texts, but then when we were at the burial site, I stepped away for a moment to look at my texts, and she informed me that Desmond would not stop throwing up and that he needed to go to the hospital. I didn't want to miss my father's repast, but I was concerned about my son, so I left.

I was relieved when the doctor's said that he had a stomach virus, and he instructed us to give him plenty of fruit juice, and to try giving him bland foods like applesauce and mashed bananas. Desmond was sitting in the back seat about to fall asleep. I was happy to be leaving the hospital because it was risky being seen with them like this. I already had to lie to my wife about why I wasn't going straight to the repast. She was understanding like always. She was secure and confident and didn't question me about that. I loved that about her, and it made it easier to do what I was doing with Naomi.

When we arrived at her apartment, Desmond had fallen asleep and I took him to his room and laid him on the bed. I exited his room and walked into the living room where Naomi was sitting on the couch. I sat beside her, she had a stressful look on her face. I put my arm around her to try to comfort her, but I was feeling stressed myself.

"It feels good when you hold me like this. You should stay a little while, I can make us something to eat." Naomi said.

I really wanted to be my father's repast, but I needed a moment to gather myself, and what better way to do that than to spend time with Naomi, and plus I was feeling guilty because my last moment with my father was an unpleasant one, and I couldn't help but feel if I hadn't confronted him then maybe he would have held on for a little longer. "That sounds good." I said.

Naomi smiled and got up from the couch and went into the kitchen. While she was fixing us something to eat, I picked up the remote off the coffee table and turned on the flat screen TV, that I had purchased for her last month and turned the channel to ESPN. I wanted to watch something to help me relax.

Forty-five minutes later, Naomi had the food ready which was baked pork chops, rolls, and macaroni and cheese. While eating out meal Valerie called me, and I sent her to voicemail. A little later she sent me a text asking me was everything alright and I sent her a quick text back telling her that it was taking a little longer than usual, and I would try to get to the repast as soon as I could, but I knew I would probably not make it. After we finished the meal, Naomi and I snuggled up on the couch to watch a movie.

Everything was going well until Naomi started complaining. "You know I want to spend more time with you like this, I wish you would make more time to visit with me and your son."

I blew out a frustrated sigh. Here I was missing my father's repast to spend extra time with her, and she was still complaining. "What do you call what we are doing right now?"

"I know, but I'm talking about during the week, and I could use extra help on the weekends, and Desmond can be a handful sometimes."

"I know, but Desmond is in daycare, and you know I have a wife."

"I know, but…." Naomi started then paused.

"But what?"

"I feel that it's unfair that you can never reveal that you're Desmond's father."

"I don't like it anymore than you do, but what other choice do I have?" Naomi was really frustrating me now because she knew all this already.

Naomi sat up straight on the couch. "I get it, but it's starting to get old, and I need more money."

I frowned. "I give you enough money."

"Well it's not enough anymore. Desmond needs a lot of new things."

"How's that when I just bought him clothes last month, and are you forgetting about this TV that I bought you." She was getting too greedy.

Naomi shrugged her shoulders. "You and Aunt Valerie have plenty of money, so I know you can afford it."

I stood up. I needed to leave now before I said something I might regret. "You're not getting anymore money out of me until next month, and I'll try to see if I can help you out more with Desmond." I said and started heading for the door.

Naomi quickly stood up and started walking after me. "Wait a minute, we didn't get to finish watching the movie."

I turned around to face her. "I'm suddenly not in the mood to finish watching it." I said sarcastically.

Naomi's face fell. "So, you're leaving just because I wanted to have a serious conversation with you."

"I also need to get going anyway. I buried my father today remember."

"Aren't you going to check on Desmond before you leave." She pleaded with me.

I didn't say anything, I just walked to Desmond's room and quietly opened the bedroom door and peeped inside. He was still sleeping soundly and then I closed the door and turned around, Naomi was standing right in front of me.

She wrapped her arms around my neck. and kissed me softly on the lips. "Please stay for a little while longer." She whispered softly.

She tried to kiss me again, but I backed away, and removed her arms from around my neck. I knew if I let her kiss me again, I wouldn't be leaving anytime soon. "I'm sorry, I can't. Maybe another time." I said and quickly left the apartment before she could protest anymore.

I was nervous as I drove home. I was driving home because I figured the repast was over by now. I was right because when I arrived home, Valerie's blue BMW was parked in the driveway. I got of my car and headed inside the house. When I closed the door, Valerie walked out of the kitchen.

"Hey, baby I was worried about you. Is everything alright with your friend's car?" she asked.

I hesitated for a second because I forgot the lie I told her, but I quickly recovered. "Yes, it took forever for me to help him get his car started. He really needs to get AAA services."

A thoughtful look passed across Valerie's face. "I'm glad you were there to help him, but it's too bad you had to miss your father's repast."

"I know I feel terrible about that, and when I left the burial site, I didn't know it was going to take that long."

"Why don't you get changed and I'll warm you up a plate." Valerie offered.

"Thanks babe." I said and kissed her on the cheek.

I went upstairs to our bedroom and took off my slacks and shirt and took a quick shower and changed into a pair of lounging pants and t-shirt. I was just about to head out of the room when Omar walked in. Both of my sons had my height and build, but their mother's complexion. Omar looked just like me while Daniel looked more like my wife.

"Hey son."

"Where were you Dad?" he asked in a sharp tone.

I stared at him for a moment because I didn't like his tone, but I didn't want to argue with him, so I answered him. "I was helping my friend fix his car, didn't your mother tell you?"

"Yes, but I don't believe that for a second. You see Naomi didn't come to the funeral because Desmond was sick, and then you just suddenly left the burial site with a lame excuse."

"What are you trying to say?"

"I think you were with Naomi all this time, and I'm wondering if Desmond is really your son." Omar said as he studied me intently.

"Watch yourself son, I already told you that nothing more happened between Naomi than a kiss, so stop trying to make this into something more than what it is." I said raising my voice.

Omar was about to say something else when Valerie entered the room. She looked back and forth between us sensing the tension. "I was coming up here to check on you Jeff, and is everything alright between you two?"

"Yes, it is, right, Omar?" I asked daring him to say something different.

"Of course, everything is fine." Omar agreed than exited the room.

"You know I'm really starting to worry about all this tension between you two. What is really going on with you guys?" she asked. My wife was a smart woman she just blindly trusted me, but I knew she couldn't keep ignoring the tension between Omar and me.

"Everything's okay between us, he's just trying finding himself that's all."

"I hope that's all it is." She said.

"Come on, I'm ready to eat that plate now because I'm starving." I said, but I wasn't really hungry because I just had a meal with Naomi. I walked out of the room with my wife following behind me. I was desperately ready to put this day behind me and I prayed that my son wouldn't give me away.

CHAPTER 6

Jeffery

Two weeks later, on a Sunday morning, I sat in the church with my wife and son Daniel as I watched Michelle step out to the podium to begin her sermon. I sat there with bitterness in my heart, wishing that it was me up there instead of her.

"Today everyone I want to talk to you about New Beginnings. When you think about new beginnings, it can be scary. Even though I am a Pastor at my own church, it was still scary to have to come back to Kansas City to take over my father's church. Sometimes when you start something new it can be uncomfortable, but you must learn to start over and embrace change. When you are faced with a change in your personal life you most often meet that change with fear. I'm going to talk today about the steps you go though and must take to go through with it.

When embracing change there are four steps that you may have to overcome. First there is the fear of failure. Success can be exciting and comfortable and can shake our world. Change is a new avenue and can lead to a lot of trial and error as an outcome. Fear of walking into failure can prevent us from embracing change. It is important not to fear failure because there is always a lot to learn to take us to the next level. Second there is the fear of pain. Quite naturally people don't want to feel the pain involved with change whether it's emotional, physical, mental, or even spiritual. Pain causes us to flee in the opposite direction. But pain is also the incitement to a strength we wouldn't know otherwise. Third there is the fear of criticism. Most people don't like change, so criticism can come as a natural result. We fear people reactions because we want their support. But what you must realize is that pleasing others instead of ourselves is setting a trap that keeps us from discovering true freedom. Fourth there is the fear of discomfort. No one likes discomfort. It can be messy, but it also can be magical. It is also where we gain the knowledge and skill for personal growth.

I want to end this by giving you six bible scriptures to help you embrace change, and those scriptures are John 14:27, "Peace I leave with you; my peace I give you. I do not give to you as the world gives. Do not let your hearts be troubled or afraid." Philippians 1:6, "He who began a good work in you will carry it on to completion until the day of Christ Jesus." Psalm 55:22, "Cast your cares on the Lord and he will sustain you; he will never let the righteous be shaken." Isaiah 41:13, "For I am the Lord your God who takes hold of your right hand and says to you, "Do not fear; I will help you." 1 Peter 5:7, "Cast all your anxiety on him because he cares for you." 2 Timothy 1:7, "For the Spirit God gave us does not make us timid, but gives us power, love, and self-discipline. Change is difficult, but we can hold firmly to the truth found in scriptures while we contest our fears. Now let's bow our heads in prayer.

I could not deny the strong presence of God in that building, and I felt God trying to work on me as well. Michelle had a natural ability to teach. She broke things down with a smooth delivery.

After the service, people started to head to the front of the church to greet Michelle, but I was headed the other way when Valerie pulled on my arm stopping me. "Come on Jeff we have to go greet your sister, she preached a terrific sermon."

Valerie knew that I wanted to lead the church, and that I resented Michelle, but I knew she was trying to keep the peace. We all went to greet Michelle, who had a nice genuine smile on her face.

When I hugged Michelle, she whispered in my ear. "Meet me in my office after I finish greeting everyone. We need to talk."

I pulled back and looked at her. I so desperately wanted to say no, but I knew my wife would encourage me to talk to her. "Sure." I said in as polite a tone I could muster. I walked over to my wife and son. "Michelle wants me to meet her in her office after she's done greeting."

"That's great." Valerie said with a smile. "Daniel and I will wait." They walked over and sat in the seats.

After Michelle was finished, I followed her to her office. Once we were inside, she sat behind the desk and I took a seat across from her.

"So, what is it that you want to talk to me about?" I asked.

"Well, we haven't really talked since I arrived back in Kansas City. I know that you're not happy that I'm leading the church, but I want you to know that I'm not the enemy.

I started laughing.

Michelle frowned. "What's so funny?"

"You telling me that you're not the enemy. When you were offered this position did you not once suggest me?"

"No, I didn't, because you know as well as I do that you are not qualified to run this church or any other church."

"And there it is; the smugness that you try so hard to hide. You have your own church, but you have to show how great you are by leading our father's church as well. You are such a show off."

Michelle stared at me in disbelief. "Is that what you think I'm doing, trying to show off?"

"Well, aren't you?"

"You're more messed up then I thought." Michelle said as if she was suddenly coming to a realization. "I'm not trying to show off. I'm honoring our father's wishes. I had to make a lot of sacrifices to do this."

I clapped my hands. "Is this what you are looking for?"

"You are unbelievable. I called you in here to try to sort out our differences but it's just no use trying to getting through to you. Not to mention how your tried to throw me under the bus at the deacons meeting last week."

"I was simply pointing out different scenarios and questions, and if you can't handle that you shouldn't be running this church."

Michelle stared at me for a moment with a sad look on her face and then said. "That will be all Jeff. You can leave my office now."

I wasted not time leaving her office. I hated that I resented my sister so much because she was a good person, but I couldn't help the way I felt, and I didn't see it changing anytime soon.

CHAPTER 7

Michelle

"That was such a great sermon you preached today." Regina said.

Regina and I were having lunch at a soul food restaurant. "Yes, I was nervous about what I should preach about, and then I just went with what was in my heart."

Regina took a sip of her tea then said. "Our children have really taking a liking towards each other."

I smiled. She was right. It didn't take long for Bradley to ask my daughter out on a date. In fact, they were on a date right now. Bradley took her to a movie after church, and then she said they probably would go out to eat afterwards. I did have my concerns because Bradley was nineteen and had his own apartment, but I trusted my daughter to not do anything she wasn't ready for. Regina told me all about the struggles she had with Bradley. She raised Bradley as a single mother because his father split shortly after he was born. She did the best she could to raise him. She got a job at a daycare and that eventually ended up with her owning her own daycare which she's had for seven years now. Even though she had her own business she had major challenges with Bradley. He ran around with the wrong crowd and she had suspicions that he had joined a gang, but over the last year and a half she said that Bradley had changed and gotten himself some new friends. He got a job at the Pepsi Cola company as a driver and was able to get his own place.

"Yes, they have and that's a good thing because now Courtney wants to stay in Kansas City. She wanted to live with Jason and his wife at first."

"Wow, I know you weren't going to have that."

"No, I wasn't. I'm glad we are settled in comfortably now." I had explained my situation to my church in Memphis. Although they were disappointed, they understood. I would check in and preach there twice a month. I was keeping my house in Memphis and I had bought a nice three-bedroom condo for us.

"That's good." She paused and then asked. "How is everything going between you and Jeff?"

I sighed. Regina knew about the tension between Jeff and me. I was still upset about the disastrous meeting we just had. Since I had been home, he tried to act like he was supportive, but I knew he wasn't. When I had a meeting with the deacons and the assistant pastor last week, he kept interrupting me and asking me these farfetched questions. After the meeting was over, I questioned him about his behavior, he said he just wanted to make sure I was fully prepared. I wasn't buying that for a second because he knows I know how to run a church. So, I thought trying to have an honest conversation with him would help, but after that meeting, he made it clear that I didn't have his support. My father left the house and most of his money to my mother, but he left Jeff and me a nice amount of money, but that wasn't enough for Jeff because he wanted to run the church too.

"It's kind of strained to be honest, but I'm sure it will get better eventually." I didn't want to talk about our meeting earlier. I wanted to forget about it.

"I hope so, because family is supposed to pull together during a time like this."

I nodded my head in agreement and we finished our lunch with pleasant conversation, and I left the restaurant and headed back home feeling good. When I arrived home, I changed into some comfortable clothes, and then decided to watch a little TV in my bedroom. I was watching TV for about twenty minutes when my cell phone rang. I picked up my cell phone off the nightstand and looked at the screen, and when I saw it was Jason calling, I sighed, then answered the call.

"Hello Jason." I said in a slightly irritated voice.

"Well hello to you too. You don't sound very happy to hear from me."

I wasn't because I knew he wanted to ask me about Courtney living with him and that wasn't going to happen. "What is it you would like to talk about? I asked in as cordial a tone as I could manage.

"I'm concerned about Courtney after she called me and told me she wanted to live with me."

"She wanted to live with you at first, but now she is happy here, and she is enrolled at the same Christian Academy that I attended."

"It's nice that you got her enrolled in school, but how can you be so sure she's happy because she hasn't been there that long."

"Trust me I'm sure. Has she called you again asking to live with you?"

Jason was quiet for a moment and then said. "Well no."

"Okay then that should let you know that she is fine, and plus she is dating someone."

"She's only been there for two weeks, who is she dating that fast?" Jason asked in a concerned tone.

Jason's tone almost made me regret telling him, but I didn't want to keep anything concerning our daughter from him.

"She's dating my best friend's son." I revealed.

"That's not good at all because if something goes wrong between them, it could affect you and your friend's relationship."

He had some legitimate concerns, but it wasn't that serious to me. "We are grown women and we aren't going to let our children dating affect us."

"Okay, but I smell trouble brewing."

I laughed. "Listen everything will be fine."

"Okay but keep me posted about this young man Courtney is dating. You know what let me speak to her about it."

"She's not here right now. She went to a movie with him. His name is Bradley by the way."

"Okay tell Courtney I want to talk to her about Bradley when she gets home."

"Will do." I said and ended the call. I continued watching TV, but for some reason Jason's concerns about Bradley and Courtney dating was starting to bother me, but I shook it off, but I couldn't ignore the funny feeling I felt in my gut.

CHAPTER 8

Jeffrey

It was a month later and I just left the house of one of my church members. Lincoln had lost his job and now he and his family was struggling. I came over to pray with him and his family because they were having a very difficult time dealing with the situation. He said it's been four months and he couldn't find another job and his savings were dwindling. I told him to keep his head up and keeping looking for a job. When his wife went into the kitchen to fix us a drink, Lincoln whispered to me that the reason he lost his job was because he was flirting with a co-worker who was receptive to it, but when he sent a lewd video to her, she got offended and showed their boss the video and he was fired. And that's why he had so much trouble finding another job. He said he wanted to tell his wife the truth but didn't know how. I was about to give him some advice on the situation, but his wife returned to the living room. I told him I would talk to him more later. Of course, my advice would be to tell his wife the truth, even though that's advice I wouldn't dare take.

I was heading home now to take my wife out to a nice dinner. We hadn't had a chance to spend time alone in a while and I was really looking forward to it. When I arrived home, I went into the den and was surprised to see my wife sitting on the couch with Desmond reading to him.

"Hey, why is Desmond here?"

Valerie looked up at me. "Oh, Naomi called me and said she had something really important to take care of this evening and she asked me to watch him for her."

I could feel my blood pressure rise. Naomi did this on purpose because I told her I couldn't spend time with her and Desmond today because I was taking Valerie out, and now she pulled this petty move. "I understand you want to help dear, but we had plans." I said as calmly as I could. I was really trying to mask my anger.

"I know but we can go out another time. Naomi needed my help, and she's a young single mom and that's tough."

I knew there was nothing I could do about the situation now. Valerie had a good heart and Naomi was taking advantage of it.

"Hey there, little man." I said to Desmond and then I held out my hand, so he could give me five. He slapped my hand.

"I'm going to cook dinner for us in a little bit, it's just going to be the three of us because Daniel is over one of his friends' house."

"You don't have to do that. I'm going to go pick us up something to eat." I said.

"That's sweet of you." Valerie said with a tired smile.

That made me even angrier. My wife was worn out from working all day, and selfish Naomi was asking her to baby-sit because she was mad at me, but I was going to give her a piece of my mind. I kissed my wife on the forehead and then left and headed to Naomi's apartment.

When I arrived there, I jumped out of my car and ambled towards her apartment. I banged on the door. I was already setting the tone. I wanted her to know how upset I was. She opened the door wearing a pair of short lounging short's that exposed her beautiful thighs and legs and a tank top.

She smirked at me. "Now is not a good time."

I ignored her comment and pushed passed her and marched into her apartment. I was about to let her have it until I saw a tall slender brown-skinned young man sitting on her couch. That made my blood boil. She had my wife baby-sitting because she wanted to get laid. "Young man you need to leave now." I demanded.

He looked at me in shock, then turned his attention to Naomi. "Naomi who is this?"

"No one important." Then she looked at me with an annoyed look on her face. "You can't come into my apartment being rude to my company."

I ignored her and then went and stood directly in front the guy. "Leave now." I said through clenched teeth.

He stood up. "I'll leave when Naomi tells me to leave." He said not backing down.

I was two seconds away from dragging him out of the apartment when Naomi got between us. "Listen Tyler maybe we should do this another time."

"Are you sure about that, because I don't think I should leave you alone with him."

"Just get out of here, no one is going to do anything to her." I didn't know who he thought he was.

"It's okay." Naomi said.

After he was finally convinced that Naomi was going to be alright, he left the house.

"Your jealousy is so hot." Naomi said in a seductive tone.

"You think this is funny, huh?"

"Yes, I sure do when you blew me off to be with your precious wife, and now you're mad because I have company."

"I'm upset because you have my wife babysitting when you knew I had plans with her." But I was also mad because she had a guy over, but I wasn't going to admit that to her.

"Forget about that. Now that you're here why don't you stay awhile." She said and started placing soft kisses on my neck.

Her soft kisses were lethal and before I knew it, I was practically snatching off those tiny shorts she had on and we had sex right there on the floor. "Wow." I said after we were done. The sex with Naomi was always amazing.

"Yes, wow is right. I'm sorry for what I did. I hate it when you blow me off. See all you have to do is give me a little more of this more often, and a little more money."

"Sweetheart you can have anything your heart desires if you keep performing like that." I said meaning it. I knew this was wrong, but it was almost impossible for me to stop now. I came over here to put her in her place, but now she had me in the palm of her hand.

Afterwards I showered and then I gave Naomi some money and she told me that she would be picking Desmond up in the morning to take him to daycare, then I left and got into my car. My cell phone was in my drink holder and I picked it up and saw I had missed calls and texts from Valerie. I had to think of some excuse to tell her for why it was taking so long to get the food. I put my phone in my pocket and headed out of the parking lot. I picked us up some food at the Italian restaurant that she loved and drove home. I got out of my car and headed inside my house. I already made up my mind to tell Valerie that the Italian place was extra crowded.

Once inside I called out for Valerie, but she didn't answer. I went into the kitchen and put the food on the counter and then headed upstairs to our bedroom where I found Valerie sound asleep. I smiled and then left the room and peeped into one of the spare bedrooms where Desmond was sound asleep as well.

I went downstairs and into the kitchen and ate my food feeling relieved that I wouldn't have to explain things to my wife tonight, but I knew that I couldn't keep having these disappearing acts without some serious explanations.

CHAPTER 9

Michelle

I was cleaning up the kitchen when the phone rang. I answered the phone.

"Hello, Pastor Roberts, this is Deacon Jermaine."

"Hi, what can I do for you? I asked curious why he called.

"I wanted to know if you would like to go out with me this weekend."

My mouth dropped wide open. I didn't know what to say. Deacon Jermaine Thompson was a handsome man. He was tall and light-skinned with a chiseled physique, but I didn't know if I should be dating anyone right now.

Deacon Jermaine laughed at my silence. "Are you still there?"

"Yes." I said finally finding my voice. "I'm flattered, but I don't know if I have time to be dating right now."

"You should make time. A beautiful woman like you shouldn't be alone forever."

I smiled. He was right. I wanted to eventually find love again, but it had to be the right situation and at the right time. If I were to say yes, where would you take me?"

"I would take you out to a nice restaurant unless there was something else you wanted to do?"

"Going out to a restaurant sounds nice." I said.

Deacon Jermaine laughed. "I take that as a yes then."

"Yes."

"Great." He said.

We decided to go out this weekend then we hung up. I stood there for a moment smiling in a complete daze until Courtney came downstairs and brought me back to reality.

"Hey mom, what's got you smiling like that?" she asked curiously.

I paused for a moment wondering if I should tell my daughter, but she would know about it anyway. "I have a date on Saturday with Deacon Jermaine."

Courtney's eyes widened in shock. "Wow, really?"

"Yes, I'm surprised myself."

Courtney looked thoughtful. "Both of us are falling in love at the same time." She said.

I narrowed my eyes at her. "Wait a minute, you're in love now?"

Courtney sighed. "You sound like dad now. He gave me an earful about Bradley."

"He's just concerned that's all, and I am to if you think you're in love." In my opinion a sixteen-year old was too young to know about love.

"I don't know if it's love, I just know when I with him my heart feels full."

I laughed. "That sounds like how I felt when I first met your dad. I know you may think you're in love, but you should slow down."

Courtney shrugged, and then she helped me finish cleaning up the kitchen. After the kitchen was cleaned, I took a shower than called Regina to tell her about my date with Deacon Jermaine. She was so excited and told me I should make sure I get my hair and nails done, and I told her I would because I had not thought about that.

The week went by fast and it was now Saturday morning and Courtney and I went to get our hair and nails done. I got caramel highlights that went good with my skin tone, and Courtney got her beautiful hair done in soft curls. After we finished getting our nails done, Courtney suggested we go shopping because she said I needed to wear something new for my date, but I knew she was only suggesting that because she wanted some new outfits too.

I picked out a nice light green dress with pumps, and I bought a couple of handbags. Courtney got a few pair of designer jeans and shoes. After shopping, we went home, and I began to get ready for my date with Deacon Jermaine. I was so nervous, he was such a handsome man, and I didn't want to do anything stupid or say the wrong things. I had been out of practice for so long. After putting on my new dress and pumps. I sprayed on some of my Vera Wang perfume. I felt a little anxious, so I said a quick prayer to calm my nerves. I reminded myself that this was just a date. Two human beings getting to know each other.

When I was finally calm, I looked myself over in the mirror, and when I was satisfied with what I saw, I grabbed my purse and went downstairs to wait for Jermaine. There was no need to call him Deacon Jermaine anymore since we were going on a date, at least when we were alone. Courtney came downstairs and told me I looked beautiful and then she was headed out to meet Bradley at the bowling alley. Her father had bought her a silver Mazda6 for her sixteenth birthday, and so far, she has been very responsible with it.

Jermaine arrived twenty minutes later dressed nicely in a pair of black pants and cream shirt. "You look beautiful, and I love the highlights." He said looking me up and down.

I smiled. "Thank you, you look handsome."

"Thank you, are you ready?" he asked politely.

"I sure am." I said and picked up my purse and we headed out the door and got into his beige Camry.

He drove us to this nice Japanese restaurant. I liked the relaxing atmosphere. The waitress seated us and took our orders. We both ordered the yakitori and we ordered ice teas to drink.

"I've been really looking forward to having this one on one time with you." Jermaine said looking into my eyes.

I blushed. "Likewise."

"So how is everything, do you feel settled in because I know this was a big change for you."

"Yes, a very big change, but I'm settling in nicely, and my church in Memphis is still doing good."

"Well if you find yourself having a hard time or need someone to talk to about anything, I'm your guy."

"That's nice of you, but I don't want to burden you with my problems." I said with a laugh.

The waitress brought us our drinks and food and we began eating. After Jermaine finished chewing his food he said. "I know, but everyone needs someone to talk to from time to time, and it's no burden at all."

His words made my heart feel warm. It was good to have some extra support because Jeff wasn't shy about letting me know I didn't have his support. "Okay, I'll keep that in mind. We were quiet for a moment while we ate our food and then I said. "So, tell me about yourself."

"Well, I'm thirty-six years old and I'm divorced. I have a six-year-old daughter, and she lives with my wife in Jefferson City."

Okay, so he was a little younger than me. I didn't mind that though. "Well, I'm divorced too, so we have that in common."

Jermaine looked thoughtful for a moment then said. "Yes, I know your divorce was all over the news, I know that had to be painful for you, living your divorce out in the spotlight."

"Yes, it was." I said recalling that very painful time in my life.

"My divorce was painful as well. I got in a car accident and suffered a horrific break to my leg, and I suffered nerve damage. I was in a lot of pain, and I had to go through a lot of physical therapy. It put a lot of strain on my marriage, and I have to admit that I wasn't the nicest person to her. So, a couple of years after my accident, our marriage was beyond repair and we got a divorce." Jermaine said.

I could understand that completely. Sometimes a marriage is beyond repair, and it's very difficult to accept that especially when you are a Christian. We finished our dinner with great conversation. I found myself really liking Jermaine and I couldn't wait to go out with him again.

CHAPTER 10

Jeffrey

Michelle was wrapping up her Sunday service, and I couldn't wait to pull Jermaine aside and ask him how their date went last night. I had blackmailed Jermaine into getting close to my sister. I needed someone to get close to her, to see if she was keeping any secrets and Jermaine was the perfect person for the job. Jermaine was young and handsome, and I knew my single and probably desperate sister wouldn't be able to resist him.

After service had ended, I told Valerie and Daniel I would meet them at home because I had some business to take care. Of course, Valerie was understanding and didn't ask any questions. I hurried out of the sanctuary and to my office. I texted Jermaine and told him to meet me in my office. He ignored my calls last night, but I wouldn't be ignored today.

I sat down at my desk and opened my laptop while I waited for Jermaine. There was a knock on the door about ten minutes later, and I knew it was Jermaine. I closed my laptop. "Please enter." I said.

Jermaine entered my office with a displeased look on his face, but I didn't care about that at all. "Please, sit." I said and pointed to the chair across from me. Jermaine slowly sat down in the chair. "So how did it go last night?" I asked.

"It went pretty good." He said vaguely.

"Come on man, I want details."

"There isn't much to tell. I had a wonderful time with your sister, and I really don't think she has anything to hide, and you should be ashamed of yourself for doing this to her."

I smirked at him. "Well, I'm not, and you shouldn't be upset about doing this at all. My sister is very green, she married the first guy that she was serious about, so it shouldn't be hard to figure out what she's hiding and she's not bad on the eyes. So, it's a win-win situation."

"What makes you so sure she's hiding something?" Jermaine asked.

I shrugged my shoulders. "I know she can't be as perfect as she pretends to be. There has to be something that I can use against her."

Jermaine shook his head. "You are a terrible person. You should be supporting your sister because she is the right person for the job.

His words angered me. "Who do you think you are to judge me. You should know all about being a messed-up person, right?"

Jermaine couldn't meet my eyes. "Look that was a while ago. I'm not into that anymore. I…"

"I have your right where I want you." I interrupted him. After Jermaine got into a terrible accident some years back, he developed an addiction to codeine. He stayed high on pills all the time, and it basically destroyed his marriage. After Jermaine picked up his daughter from daycare and drove her home while he was high, his wife Simone finally had enough and left him. That devastated Jermaine and he almost OD'd on fentanyl. I went to the doctor to see him because he put me down as his emergency contact after his wife left him. When he woke up, he confessed to me that he had been getting prescriptions from his uncle who is a pharmacist. I told him I would be there for him and help him kick his habit and I did. I got him into a program, and I never told my father about it. But after Michelle returned to Kansas City, I went to Jermaine and got him talking about all his past sins, while secretly recording him. He told me that after it rained a few weeks ago, his leg started aching, so he went and got more prescription drugs from his uncle. After I played the recording to him, he had no other choice but to go along with my plan because he didn't want his uncle to go to jail. "You have no other choice in this situation, so keep getting close to her until you find something useful out."

"But that's what I'm trying to tell you, there may be nothing useful to tell." Jermaine pleaded with me.

"Now what did you find out, because I have a feeling that you're holding back on me."

Jermaine sighed. "Look it was our first date and we are just getting to know each other, so she didn't tell me much."

"Well keep charming her until you find something useful out." I said and laughed.

"You're really disgusting man."

I was about to let him have it when my mom walked into my office. "Hello gentleman." She said with a smile, and then her smile disappeared when she noticed the expressions on our faces. "Is everything alright in here?" she asked.

"Yes, Deacon Jermaine and I were just talking, and he was just about to leave right, Jermaine?" I asked him in a tone, to let him know he better not say otherwise.

Jermaine stood up. "Yes, I was just leaving. You guys have a nice day." He said and left my office.

"Why do I have a feeling that there was a little more something to it than that." My mother said giving me the side eye.

"Oh, mom it was nothing, we were just discussing business, but what brings you by my office?"

"I wanted to know if you were coming over for Sunday dinner."

"I'm sorry I can't. Valerie is cooking today, so we are just going to have a meal at home."

A disappointed look came across my mother's face. "I just can't seem to get my two children to have a Sunday dinner with me. When I spoke with Michelle, she said she couldn't come either. I just want to have a nice meal with my children and grandchildren. That isn't too much to ask, and it's what your father would have wanted."

I looked into my mother's eyes and saw so much sadness there. I know it was hard for her living without my father. I stood up and walked over to her and hugged her. After I let her go, I said. "I'm sorry mom, I will try to make it to dinner soon."

"I hope you will because I know you and Michelle have not been speaking all that much. I know it hurts you that your father wants Michelle to run the church, but you have to accept it Jeff." My mom said as she looked at me seriously.

I felt terrible that my mother was so sad, and Michelle and I hadn't been by for dinner, but this also reminded me why I hadn't been by. I knew the conversation was going to be about me supporting my sister and how she was born for this job.

"I know mom, I will be over for dinner soon."

"Good, I'll see you later." She said and left my office.

After she left, I stayed at the church about another fifteen minutes and then I headed home. When I arrived home, I went inside and into the kitchen where Valerie was stirring a pot on the stove.

I walked up behind her and wrapped my arms around her waist and kissed her on the cheek. "That smells good, what are we having?"

"We're having some parmesan rice, and I have some ribs baking in the oven, and we're having pies for dessert."

"Aunt Valerie can I have a slice of apple pie?"

I let go of my wife and turned around to see Desmond standing in front of us. To say I was shocked would be an understatement.

"Not now, you can have some after we eat."

"Okay." Desmond said.

"Hello there Desmond." I greeted once my shock had worn off.

"Hey." He said and then he left the kitchen.

"Desmond is here again?"

Before Valerie could answer Naomi walked into the kitchen with a huge smile on her face. "Hey uncle."

"Hey Naomi, I wasn't aware that you would be joining us."

"Yes, Aunt Valerie invited me after church. I hope it's okay with you." She said with a sly smirk on her face.

Valerie turned around. "Of course, it's okay. You know you guys can eat dinner with us anytime.

I left the kitchen and went upstairs to my room and sat on my bed. I was tired of Naomi ambushing my family like this. I wanted to have dinner alone with my family and Naomi was ruining that. She needed to know her place. I stayed in my bedroom until Daniel came and knocked on the door to tell me dinner was ready.

I blew out a frustrated sigh and then I went downstairs to join my family in the dining room. The food was delicious, but I was quiet. I just listened to everyone else chat. Naomi talked how she liked working for Regina at the daycare, but she wanted a better job and was looking in to maybe enrolling in college. That would be good if she was able to get a better job then maybe she would stop hitting me up for so much money.

After dinner, I told Valerie I would bring dessert out because I was looking for any reason to leave the table. I was taking the pie out of the oven when I felt a slap on my butt. I turned around to see Naomi standing there with a flirtatious look on her face.

"Naomi, you need to stop intruding in on our family time like this." I whispered harshly.

Naomi frowned. "And Desmond and I are not your family?"

"Of course, you are, but I would rather see you guys separately, and I may have to stop seeing Desmond as much because he's talking and understanding things more and the last thing, I need is for him to slip and say something to Valerie."

"Don't worry about that, he's just a kid, and let me get a quick kiss." Naomi said.

"You're pushing it." I said and then I took a quick glance at the door before kissing her on the lips.

Naomi smiled. "See that just made my day right there."

I stared into Naomi's eyes. That's one of the reasons why I couldn't resist her. I could just give her a simple kiss and she took great pleasure in that. "Now let's get back in there before my wife gets suspicious."

Naomi winked at me. "Sure thing, but you have Auntie wrapped around your finger so she's good."

Naomi helped me with the pies, and we returned to the dining room and we all ate dessert. Occasionally Naomi would give me a sly smile. I was initially mad that she interrupted my dinner with my family, but I had to admit that I enjoyed having my cake and eating it too.

CHAPTER 11

Michelle

I woke up the next morning and took a shower and quickly dressed, then went downstairs to make a quick breakfast for Courtney and me. I had to be at the church early because I had a meeting with the women's singles ministry to discuss upcoming activities for them. It was important for me to put my full support behind them because I was single myself. Then I thought about Jermaine. Just maybe I wouldn't be single for long.

After making breakfast which was bacon, eggs, and toast, I went upstairs to check on Courtney to make sure she was up. I opened her room door and found her underneath the covers. "Courtney get up, and get dressed, breakfast is ready and I don't want you to be late for school."

When Courtney didn't budge, I walked over to her bed and pulled the covers off her. "Get up young lady!"

"Mom please stop yelling, I don't feel good."

"What's wrong, sweetie?" I asked and sat down on her bed.

"I have a stomach ache." Courtney mumbled into her pillow. She had her head turned away from me so I couldn't see her face.

I reached over and felt her forehead. "You don't feel warm or anything."

"I don't have a fever, it's my stomach and I can't go to school today."

As I looked at her, a strange feeling came over me. Something just didn't seem right, but if she said she was sick I had to take her word for it, and I didn't have time to question her about it. "Okay, I have a meeting at the church, and when I leave there, I'll bring you home some soup."

"Okay." Courtney uttered.

I left her room and was about to leave when my cell phone rang. I answered it.

"Hello, is this Pastor Michelle Roberts?"

"Yes, it is."

"Good morning, this is Bishop Phillips and I wanted to talk to you about joining our revival next month. We have four other Pastors that will be joining us."

"Wow, I would be honored to be a part of your revival." Bishop Edward Phillips was a prominent Pastor from Houston, Texas. My father had preached alongside him, but I hadn't had a chance to yet, but I was glad I had an opportunity now.

"Great, I look forward to having you here in Houston, and my condolences for the loss of your father."

I felt a twinge of sadness because I know my father would have been proud of me for preaching at a revival with Bishop Phillips. Bishop Phillips went over the details of the revival and then we ended the call.

I headed to church feeling excited. When I arrived at the church, I parked my black Cadillac XT5 and headed inside. I went to the room where the meeting was to take place. Lynn Miller, the head of the single's ministry was already there. Lynn was an attractive dark-skinned woman who was always dressed nicely. Today she was wearing a beautiful red blouse that complimented her skin tone and a knee length jean skirt with a small split on the side.

When she saw me, she smiled and said. "Good morning Pastor Roberts, I'm glad you could make it."

"Good morning, of course I was going to be here."

The room was filled up about ten minutes later along with Regina, who took a few hours off from work to attend the meeting, and then I gave Lynn the floor. "Good morning ladies, I wanted to talk to you all about having a single's retreat in Florida next year. There is another women's single ministry that's going to be there, and it would be good to fellowship with them and bounce ideas off them. We can learn from them, and they can learn from us, and while we are there it can't hurt us to enjoy the beautiful Florida weather." She said and laughed. Everyone started laughing and giving their opinions. I thought it was a good idea. I would check the church budget, but I know we had more than enough funds to finance the trip.

Everyone was talking amongst themselves when Regina's cell phone rang, she answered it and then I watched as a horrified look came across her face and she screamed out and dropped her cell phone. Everyone stopped talking and looked at her and I rushed over to her.

"What's wrong?" I asked her.

"Bradley's dead!" she screamed.

Everyone gasped. I was stunned. How could Bradley be dead? "What happened to him?" I asked her.

"I don't know." She choked out between sobs.

I picked up her cell phone off the floor because I could hear someone talking. "Hello, this is Pastor Roberts who am I speaking with?"

"Hello, Pastor this is Officer Green and, first are you a friend or family of Miss Tyson?"

"Yes, she is my best friend and she is very upset right now. What happened to Bradley?"

Officer Green was silent for a moment and then said. "Just bring her to Bradley's apartment because she is going to need someone here with her. I'll explain everything when you get here."

"Okay." I said and ended the call. One of the ladies had brought Regina a cup of water and I was thankful for that. She seemed to have calmed down a little. At least she wasn't still screaming. I gently rubbed her back. "Come on Regina, I'm going to take you to Bradley's apartment, so we can find out what happened to him, but before we go, I want everyone to bow your heads while I pray. "God please give Sister Regina the strength to deal with whatever awaits her. Keep her close to your heart and remind her that you are with her in her time of need. Amen."

Everyone repeated "Amen" in unison and I guided Regina out of the room and building and to my SUV. She gave me the directions to Bradley's house, and I prayed again silently as I drove to his apartment complex. I arrived there about five minutes later.

Bradley lived in a decent neighborhood. I parked my car in his unit and noticed a few police cars at the scene. I looked straight ahead to the apartment with the crime scene tape. Regina and I exited the car and saw an officer talking to a young man.

Regina and I walked towards them. "I'm Regina, Bradley's mother."

The officer gave us a sympathetic look. The officer excused himself from the young man and then he guided us further up the sidewalk. "Regina, your son's co-worker and manager became worried when Bradley didn't show up to work. He had a delivery first thing this morning, and when he didn't call because they say it's not like him not to show up to work, your son's manager sent his co-worker to his apartment when all his calls went unanswered. His co-worker knocked on the door and became suspicious when he saw Bradley's car here and he could hear the TV playing, he turned the door knob and the door surprisingly opened, and that's when he discovered Bradley dead from a gunshot wound to the face. He immediately called the police and now we're here trying to find out exactly what happened."

"Oh my God!" Regina screamed and began crying uncontrollably. I was overcome with emotion too."

The officer watched us for a moment until we somewhat gathered ourselves then asked. "Did Bradley have any enemies, or do you know anyone who want to hurt him?"

"No, Bradley was a good kid. He had a decent job and he goes to church."

The officer nodded his head. "Okay, it seems as if it was probably someone he knows because his door was opened and there were no signs of forced entry." The officer said and then we all turned our attention towards the apartment and where the coroners brought Bradley's body out covered with a sheet. Regina lost it and tried to run towards the body, but the officer stopped her.

"You don't want to see him like this. You should wait and view his body in the morgue."

Regina yanked her arm out of the officer's grasp. "No, I need to see my son now." Regina said with a tremble in her voice.

I put my arm on her shoulder to try to get her to calm down because her body was shaking. "Maybe he's right." I said gently.

"No, it's okay." The officer said. "Hold on a second!" The officer yelled to the coroners right before they were about to load Bradley's body in the back of their van. They stopped and turned towards us. The officer gently guided Regina to the body and I followed behind them.

When we arrived in front of the stretcher Regina took a deep breath and the coroner asked her if she was ready and she nodded yes, and they removed the sheet and I almost lost my breakfast at the sight of Bradley's face. There was a huge hole right beneath his right eye and his face was swollen, but you could tell it was him.

"My poor baby." Regina whispered, and she laid her head on top of his chest and began crying. We all waited a few minutes patiently while Regina got her emotions out and then I gently pulled her back and they loaded his body into the van.

The officer told Regina that the police department would do everything they could to bring Bradley's killer to justice and then he left. Bradley's co-worker who had been standing patiently and quietly in the corner by his apartment went over to Regina and offered her his condolences.

After everyone had left the scene, I took Regina home and stayed with her as she cried and stated her disbelief. I couldn't believe what had happened either, and then I thought about my daughter and how upset she would be about this tragic turn of events.

CHAPTER 12

Michelle

I stayed with Regina until her mother was able to come and sit with her, and then I told her I would see her tomorrow and then I headed home. On the drive home, I remembered that Courtney went over to Bradley's house last night. I fell asleep a little while after she left and when I woke up, I went to check on her and she was asleep in her room. I immediately became grateful that Courtney wasn't there when whoever shot Bradley came because she could have been a casualty. Bradley was a good kid now, but I wondered if his past came back to haunt him. Regina said that he was once in a gang and that was all behind him now, but sometimes they didn't let you walk away so easily.

When I arrived home, I called out for Courtney and when I didn't get an answer I went upstairs to her room and found her still under the covers. I turned on the light and went over and sat on her bed. I pulled the covers off her. "Courtney baby I have something very important to tell you." There was no response from Courtney she was just lying there. I shook her. "Courtney wake up."

"I'm not sleep mom." She said and turned around to face me.

I was surprised to see her eyes were almost swollen shut from crying. "What's the matter?"

Courtney's lips started trembling and she put her hands over her face. "I can't talk about it."

"Yes, you can, whatever it is you can talk to me about it." I said as I gently removed her hands from her face.

The look she gave me terrified me. She looked so lost and scared and then it occurred to me that she probably found out about Bradley already. "You know what happened to Bradley, don't you?" I asked her softly.

"Yes, because I did it." she whispered.

I froze. She couldn't have said what I thought she just said. I just stared at her.

"Please don't look at me like that, I feel horrible as it is."

"What do you mean, you did it to him?" I needed complete clarity in this moment.

"I shot him, it was an accident though. See Bradley has a gun and he showed it to me. He says he keeps it for protection because some of the guys he used to hang around still holds a grudge against him for leaving the gang. He handed me the gun. I was holding it and Bradley said I was holding it wrong, and when he was trying to show me the right way, my finger accidently pulled the trigger. I was in complete shock, I mean I had barely touched the trigger. I had blood all over my clothes and I looked down on the floor at Bradley and I knew he was dead because his eyes were staring blankly ahead. I was so scared, so I just ran and got in my car and came home. I was going to tell you what happened when I got home but you were asleep, so I took off my bloody clothes and put it in a bag along with the gun and I threw it in the trash can. "I'm so sorry I didn't mean for any of this to happen. I know I shouldn't have left him there, but I just got to this city and I didn't want to be known as a killer and I was afraid that some people wouldn't believe it was an accident."

I hugged my daughter. "Leaving him there and running was wrong, but I believe you when you say it was an accident. When Bradley showed you the gun and said he wanted to show you how to hold it, you should have refused."

"You're right, mom, and if you want me to go to the police then I will." Courtney said in a pained voice.

"No, you are not going to turn yourself in." I said surprising myself. I knew this was wrong, but I had to protect my daughter. This was my fault. She didn't want to come here, but I refused to let her live with her dad, and if I had then Bradley wouldn't be dead. I let her date him and spend so much time with him while not keeping a close enough eye on her because I was relieved that she wanted to live here with me. Then there was my position as the head of the church to think about. It would be a huge scandal in the church, and both me and Jason were well-known around the world, so this would be major news all over the world. This would ruin her life, and lastly, I thought about Jeff. He would use this situation to try to get me to step down. I didn't want to let my father down, and I know if he was here, he would want me to reveal the truth. I wanted to but I just couldn't. My friendship with Regina wouldn't be the same either way.

"Do you really believe me mom?" Courtney asked me, snapping me out of my thoughts.

"Yes, I do." I said as I could feel something stirring in my gut. I knew it was because I was going against everything I believed in, but sometimes revealing the truth could be more harmful.

I spent the next hour coaching Courtney on what she needed to tell the police because I knew they would be questioning her soon. After I felt she had everything down to the science I left her room and fixed her a bowl of soup that I discovered we already had in the cabinet. I was glad because after finding out about Bradley's death and consoling Regina I forgot to pick her up some soup. When I gave it to her, she said she didn't have an appetite, but I told her she had to eat something, and I didn't leave her room until she ate half of it.

I then took my own advice and fixed myself a sandwich because that's all I could eat, and later that night I tossed and turned all night. The next few days were a whirlwind. I was at Regina's house everyday and she was a wreck. I felt so bad comforting her when I knew what happened to her son. She was sad and angry. She wanted whoever did this to her son to pay. She asked about Courtney and I told her she was taking it hard. I allowed Courtney to stay home from school the first couple of days, but I told her she had to go to school on the third day.

The same evening after Courtney returned to school the police came by. After answering the door, I stood there looking at them in shock. I knew they were going to come by, but I guess I wasn't prepared for it to be real.

"Good evening, I'm Officer Nelson, and I'm here to see Courtney Roberts, is she available?" the stocky white officer asked politely.

"Yes, she's here." I said, and I stepped aside and let him in. Once he was inside, I shut the door behind him, and we walked into the living room. "You can have a seat on the couch, and I'll go get Courtney." I told him and then I went upstairs and knocked on Courtney's door, when she didn't answer it, I opened it and saw her lying on the bed with her ear plugs in. I knew she was listening to music. She told me that music was the only thing that kept her from being totally depressed.

Courtney removed her ear plugs. "What's going on mom, why do you look so serious?" she questioned me.

"Courtney a policeman is here to see you. Now remember everything I told you to say, and you should be just fine."

She slowly stood up. "Okay." She said simply, and we went downstairs and into the living room where Officer Nelson was sitting patiently on the couch.

Courtney sat down on the couch across from him and I sat next to her. "Hello Miss Roberts, I'm Officer Nelson and I would like to question you about the death of Bradley Tyson. We uncovered some text messages, and his last text messages were to you. There was a text message that Mr. Tyson sent you that asked if you were on your way over, and you replied that you were on your way. So, I have to ask, what exactly happened when you arrived at Mr. Tyson's apartment?"

"Actually, she never went to Bradley's apartment." I interrupted before Courtney could answer. "Courtney told me she was on her way to Bradley's apartment and I asked her if she had finished her homework, and she said she hadn't, so I told her she had to stay home to finish it."

Officer Nelson looked at Courtney. "Is this true?"

"Yes, I didn't finish my homework until late, and by then it was too late to go over to his apartment."

Officer Nelson jotted down everything Courtney said and then he asked. "Exactly what was the nature of you and Bradley's relationship?"

"We were dating"

"For how long?"

"For a little over a month."

"Do you know of anyone that would want to harm Bradley?"

"No, not at all." Courtney answered.

"Okay, well if you can think of anything that may be of help to us let me know." He said and handed Courtney his card.

"I will." Courtney said.

Officer Nelson stood up. "Thanks for speaking to me and you guys enjoy the rest of your evening." He said and left.

Courtney sighed loudly. "I was so scared. I was just waiting for him to take the handcuffs out and lock me up."

"I'm glad everything went smoothly, but if they stop by again make sure you stick to the same story. The police will notice inconsistencies."

"I hope they won't question me again, because I don't think I can take being questioned again." Courtney said then stood up and walked upstairs to her room.

Later that night I laid in bed that night staring at the ceiling. I couldn't fall asleep. I thought about my daughter and how scared she was while the policeman was questioning her. I hope that keeping this secret wouldn't slowly kill her. I lied to the police today, and I knew after this lie I told things would never be the same.

CHAPTER 13

Michelle

It was five days later, and I was at Bradley's repast at Regina's house standing in the hallway outside her bathroom door trying to convince Courtney to come out of the bathroom. I knew it wasn't a good idea to make her come to the funeral because she begged me to let her stay at home. But I didn't want anyone to get suspicious if she didn't come to the funeral. She cried her eyes out at the funeral and now she had locked herself in the bathroom.

"Courtney please come out of there." I asked impatiently. I was trying to keep it together myself. I had preached at his funeral and then had a major breakdown right after.

"I don't want to come out." Courtney said between sobs.

"Okay, let me come in and talk to you." I said as I felt a throbbing headache coming on. I had been getting these bad headaches shortly after Bradley's death." Courtney didn't respond but I heard her sobbing through the door. "Please let me in." I said. I didn't want anyone to come around the corner and overhear us.

I heard the door unlock and I quickly opened the door and went inside. I felt my heart breaking as I watched Courtney sitting on the bathroom floor. I joined her on the floor.

"Mom, I can't do this. I know you want me to go on like nothing happened, but how can I. I feel like I'm dying inside. I'm going out there and tell them what I did right now." Courtney said and stood up.

Feeling myself about to panic, I yanked Courtney down to the floor. "You will do no such thing. You will keep your mouth closed. I know this is hard for you, but you can talk to me about it. I'm here for you."

"That's not enough, and it's wearing you down as well. You broke down right after preaching."

"I know baby, but we are going to get through this somehow." I said and held my forehead. There was a shooting pain through my head so bad that my vision blurred a little. This stress was getting to me, but I had to stay strong. Both of our futures depended on staying quiet and sticking to our story.

"Mom what's wrong?" Courtney asked me with a worried look on her face.

"I'm okay, just a little headache. Nothing Tylenol can't cure."

There was a knock on the door, causing Courtney and me to jump. "Is everything alright in there?" it was Regina's mother Joyce.

"Yes, we're okay. Courtney's just feeling a little sick." I said and stood up and Courtney stood up too.

"Okay, I was just checking on you guys because I noticed you disappeared, so I figured you were in the bathroom." Joyce said.

"Yes, we will be out in a minute." I told her. Joyce said okay and I was grateful when I heard her walk away. I looked at Courtney. "Now wash your face and try to act normal and please keep quiet."

Courtney nodded and washed her face and then we left the bathroom and joined everyone in the living room. We found two chairs to sit in and Joyce spotted us and walked over to us. Joyce had the same complexion and build as Regina. She had taken great care of herself over the years.

She gave Courtney a sympathetic look. "You poor thing, I know how close you and Bradley were getting." Courtney just gave her a small smile.

Then Joyce looked at me. "It was unfortunate circumstances that brought you back to Kansas City, but I'm glad you're here because Regina really needs you and you have been a great friend to her. It's a shame that Bradley's father didn't show his face at his son's funeral." she said shaking her head.

Her words made me feel sick to my stomach. I didn't deserve her praise. "I'm more than happy to be there for her." I forced out. Then I looked around. "Where is Regina?"

"She went to go lie down, your mother went to talk to her."

I wanted to go upstairs and check on Regina, but I knew my mother was doing an excellent job comforting her, and plus I didn't want to leave Courtney alone. She had already threatened to tell them everything.

I chatted for a few more minutes with Joyce. She told me how much she was going to miss Bradley. He was her only grandchild. This made me feel even worse and then we left after I told everyone that Courtney needed to get home because she was sick. On the drive home there was complete silence. My daughter and I were both a mess and didn't know what to say to each other at the moment.

CHAPTER 14

Jeffrey

It was two weeks after Bradley's funeral, and everyone was at my mother's house for Sunday dinner. She was happy that everyone finally decided to have dinner with her. It was initially supposed to be me and my family and Michelle and her family, but my mom extended the invitation to Regina because she needed to be surrounded by people who cared about her.

Everyone had just fixed their plates and we were sitting around the dining room table. I looked at the head of the table at my father's empty seat and I felt sad that he wasn't here with us. I still regretted that moment in the hospital with my father and I wanted to confess that moment to my wife so many times, but I didn't. I knew my father would be ashamed at my action and behavior towards my sister, but I just couldn't help it. I wanted to carry on his legacy even though Michelle was so much better suited for the job, but as I looked at Michelle sitting at the table with a fake smile plastered on her face and the somber look on my niece's face, I knew there was something wrong with this picture. I know they were upset about Bradley's death, we all are, but something more seemed to be going on with them. Michelle just wasn't herself. She preached at Bradley's funeral and she broke down crying uncontrollably right there in front of everyone. She held it together better at my father's funeral. Something was off, my gut was telling me this, and I needed to know what was going on and I had been harassing Jermaine about finding something out. He told me that Michelle hadn't wanted to go out since their last date, and I told him he had to be more persistent. I was determined to find some dirt out on Michelle; the sooner the better.

"I'm am very pleased to have my family here with me today." My mother said.

"I told you mom we were going to have dinner with you." I said.

My mom smiled at me and it was a genuine smile. Everyone made small talk as we ate my mother's delicious meal, well everyone except Michelle and Courtney. I know that no one wanted to talk about anything too heavy because of what happened to Bradley, but I was going to use this time to put my sister on the spot.

"What's going on sis, you are really quiet? I asked in a taunting voice." Michelle stopped eating and looked at me and my mother narrowed her eyes at me, and Valerie gave me a disappointed look.

"I'm eating if that's alright with you." Michelle snapped.

I smirked, and there it was. I had struck a nerve, now all I needed to do is push just a little further and see if I could get her to break. "I just wanted to ask if you're alright. Why are you acting so defensive; it's like you're hiding something?

"Jeff stop it." Valerie said sternly.

"Come on babe, you know it's not like that. I'm just checking on my sister."

"Checking on me, please. You just want to see me fail that's all. It's not my fault that you're not good enough to run the church." Michelle fired back.

Her comments made me furious. "You always thought you were better than me, but you're not. If anyone bothered to pay attention, they could see that something is not right with you." I spat out.

"Leave my mother alone!" Courtney screamed shocking everyone including myself.

"Calm down sweetie." Regina said calmly as she put her hand on Courtney's shoulder.

"No, I will not sit here and listen to you bully my mother. What kind of older brother are you?" Courtney asked hotly.

"Mom, I'm sorry but we're going to leave now." Michelle said standing up. She was talking to my mother, but she was staring directly at me. "Jeff being the immature jerk he is has upset my daughter, so I'm leaving."

"No stay, we need to talk about this as a family. Running away will not solve anything." My mom pleaded with us.

But her words fell on deaf ears because Michelle, Courtney, and Regina left the house, and once they left, I was in the hot seat.

"Why did you do that dad?" my son Daniel asked me. He was looking at me as if he didn't recognize me. Daniel was usually laid back so him questioning me surprised me.

"Listen I didn't mean to ruin everybody's evening, but my questions were legitimate. She's behaving weirdly if you guys would just pay attention."

"You need to get all this jealousy and hatred out of your heart because it will only lead you down a path of destruction. God don't like it when you mess with his anointed, so tread carefully son." My mom said.

Her words just went in one ear and out the other. She was talking about Michelle as if she was a saint and I wasn't buying it. Little Miss Perfect was hiding something, and I was definitely going to find out what it is.

We finished our dinner with awkward conversation. After they left, there was thick tension in the room that not even a chainsaw could cut through. When we finished eating, I hugged my mother and apologized to her and we headed home.

When we arrived home, Valerie gave me the silent treatment. I was laying back on the bed waiting for her to get out of the shower. I was tired of her ignoring me. After she finished her shower, she put lotion on her body and put on a pretty, lavender silk nightgown and climbed in bed beside me. She was looking good and smelling good, so I pulled her body close to me, but she was resistant.

"Come on, are you going to keep punishing me?"

"You should be ashamed of yourself for behaving that way, and in front of Daniel, what kind of example are you setting? You don't want your son trying to push around women, do you?"

"I wouldn't call it pushing her around, I would call it calling her out on her crap."

"I noticed that Michelle was quiet and distracted, but she was deeply affected by Bradley's death and so is Courtney. You should support your sister. She earned the right to head your father's church."

I sighed. I knew she earned the right, but I still didn't like it. "He should have left me in charge. I'm his first-born son." I said feeling myself becoming tense.

Valerie wrapped her arms around me and kissed me softly on the cheek. "You are so tense. Lay on your stomach."

I didn't hesitate to do as my wife said. My wife began gently massaging my back and shoulders and it felt incredible. Moments like this made me realize why I loved my wife so much. Her massages were lethal. I closed my eyes and let out a soft moan.

"Baby I know you don't like your sister being in charge, but you have to get over it because your behavior at dinner was unacceptable."

"You're right." I mumbled softly. I would try to lay off Michelle at least in front of everybody, and I still had Jermaine working for me.

After Valerie finished giving me a massage, we made love and afterwards I held her in my arms and just before drifting off to sleep I remember thinking of how much I loved my wife and needed to do better by her.

CHAPTER 15

Michelle

I was sitting on the bed in my bedroom going over my notes for the sermon I was going to be preaching for the revival, but I couldn't concentrate because I was beyond exasperated with Jeff. It took me a while to calm myself down enough to even go through my notes. When I took Regina home all she talked about was how much of a jerk my brother was and how he wished he could be as good as me, and that made me feel even more culpable. The main reason I was so upset with Jeff is because he was right. I was hiding something, and I hated that he was able to see it. He took me out of character, and I abhorred that. He sent Courtney who was barely hanging on by a thread into a rage. She immediately went to her room when we arrived home. I loved my brother, but I needed some serious space from him, but that was impossible since we had to work together at church.

I continued going over my sermon notes until I heard the doorbell ringing. I was dressed in my pajamas, so I just slipped on my bedroom shoes and trotted downstairs and answered the door.

I was surprised to see Jermaine standing at the door. "What are you doing here?" I asked.

"I just came by to check on you."

"Thanks, but you didn't have to do that because I'm fine."

"No, you're not fine. I can tell just by looking at you. You looked stressed out and like you haven't had a good night sleep in days." He said taking in my appearance.

I felt slightly insulted, but he was telling the truth. I hadn't had a good night sleep since I lied to the cops. I just stood there looking at him not knowing what to say.

"So, are you going to let me in or what?" Jermaine asked with a smile.

I started to say no, but if I didn't let him in, I knew I would just go upstairs to my room and read over my sermon notes that I couldn't concentrate on. I really needed the distraction. "Sure, come on in." I said as I stepped aside to let him in.

Jermaine walked inside, and I shut the door behind him, and we walked into the living room and sat down on the couch. "What's going on, Michelle?"

I sighed. "I'm having one of those days. Our family was having a nice family dinner until my brother ruined it with his shenanigans."

An unreadable expression came across Jermaine's face and he studied me for a moment before saying. "You know what if talking about this is going to upset you, let's talk about something else."

I smiled because I really didn't want to talk about Jeff. "Well before you came over, I was going over my notes for the revival, but I just can't seem to get my sermon together. I'm thinking about calling Bishop Phillips and telling him I can't make it."

"You shouldn't do that, I'm sure whatever it is you can work through it."

"I don't think so; my mind is just not into it."

"You have to get your mind into it, I'll even go with you for moral support and to keep you company in Texas."

I grinned. "Now Jermaine you know that's not a good idea."

"Why not, we're both adults. We can handle taking a trip together without crossing any lines."

I looked at his handsome face. It would be hard to resist him. I hadn't been with a man in that way since Jason. I stayed busy and didn't really think about it until now. How could I not think about it when a handsome man like Jermaine was sitting across from me. Having Jermaine accompany me on the trip was exactly what I needed.

"Sure, I would love for you to come with me, it's in two weeks."

"Great." He said.

We watched TV together for about an hour and then Jermaine left. I checked on Courtney. She was asleep, so I went to my room to try to do the same. I managed to get a little sleep. The next morning, I got up and dressed and I went to Courtney's room to make sure she was up. She was sitting on her bed putting on her shoes.

"I can make you some breakfast if you're hungry."

"No, I'm not hungry."

"You have to eat." I told her.

"I'll grab an apple or something."

"Okay, and there are some Ensures in the refrigerator."

Courtney nodded her head and I exited her room feeling helpless. My child was under some serious strain and stress and I know I was of no help convincing her to withhold the truth. I went to the kitchen and ate a bowl of cereal, and Courtney came downstairs a few moments later and grabbed an apple and a bottle of Ensure. She waved good-bye and headed to school.

I was going to take care of some business at church and then stop by the daycare to have lunch with Regina. I was glad she was back at work, but she told me she wouldn't have real peace until Bradley's killer was found. On the news they said they had no leads, but the cops said they suspected an old member of the gang he used to be a part of.

After finishing my cereal, I headed to the church and to my office. I went through my emails because I had a ton of them that I hadn't looked through yet. An hour later, I had gone through half of them when my cell phone rang. I answered it.

"Hello, may I speak with Ms. Roberts."

"Yes, this is Ms. Roberts speaking."

"Hello, this is Principal Walden at Waller's Christian Academy and I want to talk to you about Courtney."

"What's going on?" I asked becoming very worried.

"Courtney's in the Guidance Counselor's office because she won't stop crying. Her teacher said that she has been very sullen lately, but today she just broke down and the crying won't stop."

"Say no more, I'll be right there." I said and headed out of my office.

My assistant Ciara was sitting at her desk. "Is everything alright Pastor?" she asked noticing my mood.

"I have to go to school and pick up Courtney. I probably won't be back today, so just cancel any appointments I have for today or direct them to Pastor Dan if it's okay with them." I said and hurried down the hall and out of the building. I quickly drove to the Academy and went to the Guidance Counselor's office.

"Hello, Pastor Roberts, I'm Rhonda Hill the guidance counselor. It's nice to meet you in person, but I'm sorry that it has to be under these circumstances." She said and extended her hand for me to shake."

I shook her hand. Rhonda was an attractive light-skinned tall black woman. I looked around her office expecting to see Courtney. "Where is Courtney?" I asked.

"She went to the bathroom. Please have a seat." I sat down in the tan chair and she sat down in the chair across from me.

"Courtney has said she's upset about the death of a young man she was dating."

"Yes, she is."

Rhonda nodded in understanding. "I can understand that, but I think that maybe she needs to see a grief counselor or something."

"Perhaps you're right." Courtney's grief was now uncontrollable, but I knew that the only thing that would help her to fully heal was to admit the truth, and I didn't want her to do that, so I would go with the option of talking with a grief counselor.

Rhonda printed off some sheets to give me information on certain grief counselors, and when fifteen minutes passed by and Courtney still hadn't returned from the bathroom, I became worried. "Excuse me, I'm going to go to the bathroom to check on Courtney." I said and left the office.

I remembered exactly where to bathroom was. When I arrived at the bathroom, it was empty, and I knew that my daughter had probably left the school premises. I looked under the stalls to make sure and no one was in them. Now I was angry, the guidance counselor shouldn't have let Courtney out of her sight when she was so clearly distraught. I stormed out of the bathroom and down the halls and back into the office.

"My daughter is not in the bathroom. You shouldn't have let her out of your sight when she was so upset. You should have waited until I was here so I could accompany her." I said angrily.

Ms. Hill was taken aback by my tone. I was normally very polite, but my distraught daughter was missing so being nice wasn't on the menu.

"I'm sorry, but I didn't want to keep her from using the bathroom."

"I'm going to look outside for her car, and you check around the school to see if she is still here." I said and quickly left the building.

When I arrived at the students' parking lot, I searched around and didn't see her car. She had left, and I needed to look for her. I jogged around the building and to my car and left the school. I took my cell phone out of my pocket and put it on speaker and called Courtney. It rang and rang, and then finally went to voicemail. I called again, and it went straight to voicemail. I hit the steering wheel in frustration. "Where are you Courtney." I said out loud.

I didn't know where to go so I went home, hoping she would be there. As soon as I arrived home, I called out for Courtney, and when she didn't answer I ran upstairs and checked all the bedrooms and she wasn't in any of them. I went downstairs and plopped down on the couch in frustration. I tried to gather myself. I needed to be thinking clearly, so I can plan my next move. I was sitting there thinking for about ten minutes and when the door opened, I quickly shot up off the couch.

Courtney walked in the living room slowly with a vacant look on her face. I ran to her and hugged her tight. "Baby you scared me half to death, don't ever do that again." I said as I held on to her. I let her go and sat down on the couch and Courtney sat next to me.

"I'm sorry mom, I went to Bradley's grave. It's the only thing that could make me feel better. I never got a chance to really say good-bye to him and apologize for ending his life. I couldn't really say what I wanted at his funeral because everyone was there."

I looked at my daughter's face that was stained with dry tears and I knew I had to do something drastic. I took her hand. "I'm sorry you had to go through that, but it was an accident always remember that." And I took a deep breath because I couldn't believe what I was about to say next. "I think you should go live with your father."

Courtney's eyes widened. "Are you serious, you don't want me here anymore."

"No, of course I want you here, but being here may be too much for you. You will be constantly reminded of what happened to Bradley."

"You're right, but no matter where I'm at, it won't stop me from thinking about what happened."

"I know, but I still think moving to California with your father would be best."

Courtney nodded her head as tears streamed down her face. I took Courtney's hand in mine and told her to close her eyes while I prayed for her. I hoped that God showed His grace for my daughter.

CHAPTER 16

Michelle

Two weeks later Courtney and I were taking a cab to Jason and Leslie's LA home. I had called Jason as soon we landed, and he offered to pick us up from the airport, but I told him we would catch a cab.

When we arrived, Jason opened the door and came out and helped us take Courtney's luggage inside his mansion. His home was extravagant. Jason and Leslie certainly didn't hold back when picking out their home. I remember after their wedding, they did a TV special showing everyone around their home. I loved the Olympic sized pool in their backyard.

Once inside, I sat down on the tan suede couch, while Jason took Courtney's luggage to her room, and Courtney followed behind him to get settled in. Jason returned about ten minutes later and joined me on the couch.

"Well, you're certainly looking good Michelle. Those highlights look good on you." He said taking in my appearance. I was wearing blue jeans and a red blouse.

"Thank you, you're looking good too." And he did. Jason had taken great care of himself over the years. Jason studied me intently and I was becoming uncomfortable under his stare. "Why are you staring at me?"

"I'm waiting for you to tell me what's really going on."

"It's like I told you over the phone Courtney is having a difficult time dealing with Bradley's death, and I feel that she needs to be away from all of it."

"And that's it?"

"Yes, why are you questioning this. Isn't this what you wanted, for Courtney to be here with you?"

"Indeed, it is, but something just seems off about all of this."

"You're reading too much into this." I said nervously.

"Michelle, you look great, but I can see the worry behind your eyes. I know you very well, and I know when something is going on with you. You were never the type of person to ask for help, but it's okay to ask for help. I'm still here for you." He said and took my hand into his.

I looked into his eyes and I wanted so badly to tell him the whole story, but I just couldn't do it. He was Courtney's father, but I felt that I was handling it the best way I knew how, and if I involved him things would just get too messy. I was about to tell him I was fine when Leslie walked in. Leslie is a gorgeous woman, she reminded you of a slightly darker Mariah Carey.

She looked down at Jason holding my hand and asked. "Am I interrupting anything?"

I knew that Jason and I holding hands slightly bothered her because there was still a natural chemistry between us.

Jason let go of my hand. "No, me and Michelle were just talking about Courtney."

Leslie looked back and forth between Jason and me and then said. "It's good to see you Michelle, where is Courtney?"

"It's good to see you too and Courtney is upstairs getting settled in." I told her.

"I'm going to enjoy having her here. I'm going to go check on her. She gave us one final looked and then went upstairs.

I watched her until she disappeared upstairs. I knew how much she loved Courtney and I appreciated that. I remember right after she and Jason were married, she talked about how ready she was to have kids, but it never happened, and I couldn't help but wonder if she had some fertility issues or if they had changed their minds. I never asked because I felt it wasn't my place or buisness.

"I think I better be going now." I said and stood up.

"You don't have to rush off. You just got here, besides where would you go? Have dinner with us."

He was right I didn't have anywhere to go, but it was LA and I'm sure I could find some places to go to. I planned to stay here for a couple of days before flying out to Texas for the revival. "Okay, I will stay for dinner."

Later we had a delicious pasta dinner made by their Chef. Courtney's mood seemed to be better and I could already see that her being in LA was going to be a positive change for her. I had already had her records from school transferred to a Private School here in LA.

After dinner I left and checked into the hotel. I called Pastor Dan and asked him how everything was going, and he told me not to worry that he had things under control until I returned to Kansas City.

Over the next few days I had fun in LA, I took Courtney shopping and let her know that she could always call me if she needed anything. Finally, my days were up in LA and I took a plane to Houston, Texas. When I arrived, I booked a hotel room, and then had lunch with Bishop Phillips and the other Pastors. This revival was going to be about faith and prosperity. I had managed to finish my sermon, I just hoped my delivery would be good because I was feeling off these days.

After the lunch I went back to my hotel room. Jermaine called me and told me that he would be arriving the next afternoon, and I was excited about that because he would get to see my sermon. My headache had started up again, so I took a couple of Tylenols and my headache subsided. I took a relaxing bath and went to bed.

The day of the revival I arrived at the church feeling like a ball of nerves. It was my turn to go on next, and when my name was announced the congregation cheered loudly. I smiled as I walked out and stepped behind the podium. The congregation stood up and clapped for me. I could see it in their eyes how excited they were to see me, but I felt like a fraud that didn't deserve to be there. I had to shake those feelings off because I had a sermon to preach.

As I preached the crowd cheered and yelled amen, I knew it was good, but I just didn't feel it in my heart. The lie that I told and the secret I was keeping was hindering me greatly. The congregation loved my sermon, but that joy and peace that I felt after preaching was not there.

After I finished, I left and watched the other Pastors preach, when they finished, I headed back to my hotel room and kicked off my heels and sat down on the couch. I was about to call room service when there was a knock on my room door. I walked to the door and looked through the peephole, and my heart skipped a beat when I saw Jermaine standing there. I quickly opened the door.

"Hello, that was an excellent sermon you preached. I feel richer already."

I laughed. "Thank you." I said and stepped aside so he could enter. I shut the door behind him, and I went and sat on the couch and Jermaine joined me.

"I was just about to order room service, you want some?" I asked.

"Sure, because I am starving. I arrived here a little before your sermon started and I skipped eating because I didn't want to miss your sermon."

I went and got the menus out of the kitchen and we both decided on the steak and scalloped potatoes with red velvet cake for dessert. We ordered raspberry teas to drink. Our meal arrived twenty minutes later, and we went into the kitchen area to eat.

"This steak is really good." Jermaine said as he took a bite of his steak.

"Yes, it is." I said distractedly. I was still bothered about my lack of peace after my sermon.

"Are you okay, because I would think you would feel on top of the world after bringing the house down like that."

I shook my head sadly. "I'm glad everyone got what they needed from it, but I don't have any peace." I confessed. I was tired of pretending.

Jermaine stopped eating and gave me a serious look. "You should tell me what's bothering you because I'm here for you."

I looked into Jermaine's eyes and I felt he was being genuine, so I decided to be candid with him. I closed my eyes before speaking because if I had to look at him while saying this I didn't know if I could go through with it. "My daughter accidently shot and killed Bradley, and I lied to the police and told them my daughter was with me that night." I revealed, then I slowly opened my eyes and looked at him.

Jermaine was looking at me with his mouth wide open, and for a moment I regretted telling him until he began speaking. "Wow, I definitely didn't expect that, but I can understand why you did what you did. Any parent would try to protect their child at any cost."

I felt relieved. "I'm glad you understand and for a moment I felt that I was causing my daughter more harm than good because she seemed to be on the verge of a nervous breakdown, but she seems better now that she is living in LA with her dad. It's so hard living with this and facing my best friend."

"I know it's hard to keep this from your best friend, but your daughter comes first, and I'm glad Courtney is feeling better, and you're not the only one that hasn't been totally truthfully about everything. I told you that my wife and I are divorced, but I wasn't entirely honest about why. After my accident, I developed an addiction to prescription pills, and I was high a lot and one day I was high while driving around with my daughter and that was it for my wife."

I was stunned at his revelation, but I sure that I beat him with my confession. "You were in a lot of pain so that's understandable, but are you still addicted?"

A sheepish look came across Jermaine's face. "I had a set back a couple of months ago, but I threw the bottle away and didn't take any."

"Are you in constant pain?"

"Sometimes, especially when it rains."

"Well we both have things we have to learn to deal with." I said.

After finishing our meal, we watched TV and I rested my head on his shoulder. I was glad Jermaine was proving to be a man that I could count on.

We had been watching TV for a while when I felt a sharp pain in my head that caused me to cry out. This time it was worse.

"Are you alright?" Jermaine asked.

I was trying to respond to him, but I couldn't say anything, and he became blurry and I fell back on the couch and passed out.

CHAPTER 17

Michelle

I woke up in the hospital with Jermaine standing over me with a nervous look on his face. I squinted my eyes at him because my vision was blurry. It took me a moment to remember everything. But I finally remembered having a sharp pain in my head before passing out.

"Thank God you're awake; you scared me. I'm going to go get the doctor."

A moment later, a middle-aged blond white man walked into the room. "Hello, Ms. Roberts I'm Dr. Nielson and I'm a neurosurgeon that will be handling your case. I understand you passed out. Can you describe to me how you were feeling before you passed out?"

"Yes, I felt a sharp pain in my head, and my vision blurred, and I couldn't speak."

Dr. Nielson nodded his head. "Yes, I think you were having some type of seizure, and I want to get a head CT just to see what's exactly going on."

His words frighten me. *I was having a seizure?* I thought I was having headaches because of the stress I was under, I never expected to have something wrong with me.

Dr. Nielson noticed my expression and quickly tried to give me positive words. "Just relax. Don't worry yourself until we know everything." He said gently. "I'll be right back with a few other doctors to get you to your CT." He left the room.

Jermaine squeezed my hand. "Don't worry I'll be right here with you."

"How am I supposed to relax and not worry when I may have had a seizure, and something may be wrong with my brain."

"Trust in God." Jermaine said and took my hands and began to silently pray.

Tears spilled down my cheeks. I should have been praying and normally the first thing I would do is pray, but I felt so out to sync with God.

The doctors came back in my room about ten minutes later and took me to get a head CT. I felt uncomfortable and claustrophobic having to go inside that little machine. But I managed to stay calm and get through it. I was so relived when I finally got out of that machine.

The doctors took me back to my room and Jermaine and I made small talk as we nervously waited for the results. When we ran out of things to say we watched TV while we were both in deep thought. Dr. Nielson came back to the room about two hours later with a grim look on his face and my heart dropped in my stomach because I knew it wasn't going to be good news.

"Ms. Roberts your CT results show a tumor in your brain that is very close to your optic nerve. That explains your headaches and blurred vision. It's a benign tumor and can be removed, but by it being so close to your optic nerve there is a chance that you could lose your vision."

I immediately started crying. A life without vision? I couldn't imagine it. Was this my punishment for lying to the cops and making my daughter withhold the truth. That made me cry even harder and Jermaine wrapped his arms around me. After I had gathered myself, I looked at the doctor.

"Is there any chance that the tumor will go away on it's on?" I couldn't stand the thought of someone cutting into my brain.

"We can give you some medicine to shrink it, but you will risk it still growing and further invading your optic nerve. We need to surgically remove now before it's too late and you completely lose your vision."

"But you said I can lose my vision with the surgery."

"I know but having surgery is your best option. I can schedule your surgery now, and we can have an operating room ready in an hour."

I sat there for a moment trying to figure out what I should do. I looked at Jermaine for guidance.

"It's your decision but I think surgery would be best."

I nodded in agreement. I knew it was best to handle the problem now instead of waiting. "Schedule the surgery." I told Dr. Nielson before I changed my mind.

"I will handle that now." Dr. Nielson said and quickly left the room. He seemed relieved that I decided to have the surgery.

"I turned to look at Jermaine. "Call my mother and tell her but tell her not to tell Courtney yet." I didn't want her to have to deal with anymore bad news right now.

"Sure thing." He said and pulled out his cell phone.

I gently grabbed his hands. "No, wait until I'm in surgery first."

"Are you sure about that because I'm sure she would want to talk to you first."

"I know she will. I can't talk to my mother because she might breakdown."

Jermaine agreed to not call my mother until after I was in surgery, but I could tell he disagreed with that.

Dr. Nielson came into my room along with two other doctors and they wheeled me to the operating room. Just before they put me under anesthesia, I prayed to God that everything would go well with my surgery.

I woke up with my mother and Jermaine standing over me and tears of joy slid down my face because I knew God had answered my prayers.

"Michelle, I'm so happy you're finally awake." She said in a voice filled with so much emotion.

"I'm so happy I can see." I said in a weak voice. My head hurt tremendously.

My mom and Jermaine laughed at my words and then Jermaine went to go get the doctor.

Dr. Nielson came in and checked my vitals and asked me other questions and he determined I would be just fine, and that I would have to stay in the hospital for only a week. That was music to my ears.

Jermaine stayed with me for about twenty minutes and said he had to go back to his hotel for a little while and then he would be back.

My mother and I were now alone. "I'm glad that Jermaine was here for you. I know you must have been scared."

"I was, I thought I would never see again."

"I was scared too. It made me think of your father. I was hoping you wouldn't develop brain cancer or something."

"Please don't even think that."

"I know, I quickly got rid of that thought as soon as it came to my mind. Your brother was very worried about you. Which reminds me that I have to call him to let him know how your surgery went."

I was a little surprised that my brother was so worried about me, but I knew he loved me even though he had a funny way of showing it.

"I know what you're thinking but Jeff loves your very much. He just has to get over all this bitter and resentment he has. But on a lighter not. You need to keep seeing Jermaine because I can tell that man loves you. I could see it with the way he was worried about you during your surgery. He is a keeper."

I smiled. Jermaine didn't judge me when I told him the truth about what happened to Bradley. Yes, he was definitely a keeper.

CHAPTER 18

Jeffrey

It was about noon and I was headed to Naomi's house to surprise her since she took the day off to take care of some errands, and Desmond was in daycare. I originally told her that I couldn't see her since I had a meeting this morning, but I finished up early, so I was going to go see her now.

As soon as I parked in the parking lot of Naomi's apartment complex my cell phone rang. I parked my car then answered my phone, it was Jermaine. I was glad he finally called me back because I was very curious to know what went on with him and Michelle at the revival. It had been a couple of weeks since the revival and Michelle was doing well after her surgery. I was very relieved she was alright but that didn't change my mission of getting dirt on her. Hopefully he had some useful information.

I answered the call. "Hey, did you find out anything?"

"I have something to tell you, but I think it would be best if I tell you in person."

Now my interest was really piqued. "Why can't you tell me now?"

"Because I rather tell you this face to face."

"Stop being so dramatic and tell me." I said. I didn't understand his need to make me wait.

"I have to go now, maybe I can stop by your house later or we can meet somewhere." Jermaine offered.

"Okay." I reluctantly agreed.

We ended the call and I exited my car and went up to Naomi's apartment. I knocked on the door and when a minute went by and she still hadn't answered the door I knocked again. She still didn't answer the door. I knew she was home because her car was there. I had a replay in my mind about her having a guy in there the last time she didn't answer the door, but I knew she couldn't have a guy in there when she asked me to come over, but I did cancel on her, so it was possible. I was tired of having this silent debate in my mind, so I took out my keys and found the spare key to her apartment and unlocked the door. I went inside and looked around. No Naomi. I figured she was in her bedroom, so I took quick strides to her bedroom. Her bedroom door was cracked open, so I looked through it and saw her and a guy sound asleep under the covers.

Looking at her underneath the covers with that guy, had me irate. Just what kind of game was Naomi playing. I pushed the door open with force and the door hit the wall with a loud thud stirring them awake.

They both looked at me in shock and I recognize the guy as Tyler. "You can't come over here like this unannounced." Naomi said after she got over her shock. She clutched the blanket tightly over her.

Tyler laughed. "Old dude, what is your problem. You can't handle a young hot thing like Naomi anyway, and you should be home with your wife anyway."

I looked at Naomi, furious that she had told this guy my business. "Old man, huh." I marched over to him and dragged him out of the bed with him dressed in boxers and slammed him against the wall so hard a picture fell off the wall. I put my forearm tightly against his neck. Tyler's eyes went wide with shock. "I suggest you take your ignorant behind out of this apartment and watch your mouth before I put you in the hospital."

"Jeff stop it!" Naomi exclaimed.

I stared into Tyler's eyes, making sure he got the message before I let him go. He looked scared like the punk he really was, so I let him go.

Tyler scrambled to put on his jeans and shirt and then before he left, he looked at Naomi and said. "Look, I'm tired of all this. Call me when you get tired of this old head playing you." He said and left the room quickly.

"See look what you did." Naomi said with a dismal look on her face.

I didn't like that look at all because it told me that she really like this guy. "Are you in love with that clown?"

"He's not a clown and what difference does that make, you love your wife don't you?" she asked sarcastically as she removed the covers off her. She was wearing only a bra and panties and her curly hair was in disarray. She got up and put on a pair of shorts and t-shirt and left out of the room.

I followed her as she walked into the kitchen. "If you are in love with this dude, then he needs to be helping you with your bills." I didn't like the fact that she was dismissing me.

Naomi went to the refrigerator and took out a bottle of juice and went into the cabinet and took out a glass and poured the juice and took a sip. She then turned around and looked at me. "I'm tired of all this. We make plans and then you cancel, and then you get mad and jealous because someone else was over here. I want to be done with all this."

"Just what are you saying?" I questioned as I walked over to her and stood directly in front of her. I didn't love Naomi, but I had feelings for her, and I definitely didn't want to stop what we were doing.

Naomi took another sip of her juice and then stared into my eyes with laser focus. "I don't want to keep sneaking around like this. I'm only twenty-one years old, I deserve to have a life and someone who really loves me; not be tied down to a married man. I'm going to tell Aunt Valerie everything."

I knew she was serious, and her words had my heart pumping so fast, that if you lifted my shirt you probably could see the imprint of it on the outside of my chest. "You are not going to tell my wife anything." I spat out.

"You always tried to control me, but you can't control this. Like it or not I'm telling her."

"No, you are not." I said and grabbed her arm causing her to drop her glass of juice on the floor. The glass broke spilling juice on the floor.

"Let go of me!" Naomi shouted and tried to yank her arm away from me, and when she did that she slipped down on the spilled juice and fell backwards hitting the back of her head on the edge of the stove. I heard a crack.

I stepped back in complete shock. I looked at her seemingly lifeless body. I felt for a pulse. She had one. I stood there for a moment wondering what I should do next. I wanted to call for help, but then I would have to explain what happened and I didn't want Valerie to find out I was over here. Since she had a pulse, I figured she would wake up and be alright, she would be disoriented that's all.

My mind was made up. I was leaving, and I quickly hurried out of her apartment looking around to see if anybody was watching me. Luckily no one saw me. It was the middle of the day when most people were working or in school.

I hurried out of the parking lot and headed home, there was nowhere else I needed to be since my church business had been taken care of for the day. When I arrived home, I made me a sandwich and watched TV, but it was hard for me to focus because my mind was on Naomi. I hoped she had woken up. When Daniel got home from school, he asked me if he could go to the library with his friend because he had to work on a project for school, and I told him it was okay, and gave him some money so he could get something to eat with his friend. I continued to watch TV until the telephone rang. I answered it.

"Hey honey, I'm going to be a little late. The daycare called and told me Naomi never came to pick up Desmond. I'm going to go pick him up and then stop by her apartment to check on her. This is not like her at all."

"Okay, babe, I'll see you when you get here." I said as calmly as I could because inside, I was going crazy with worry. "I'm sure she's fine." I said out loud. *But how could she be fine when she didn't pick up Desmond?*

I just sat there nervously, blankly looking at the TV, until the phone rang about twenty minutes later. I stared at the phone a few seconds before answering it because I felt it in my gut that Valerie was calling me with bad news. I finally answered the phone.

"Jeff, there's been an accident. I found Naomi on her kitchen floor. She was awake but can't move or speak. It's horrible, she's been lying here soaked in her urine for hours. There's some spilled juice on the floor, so I surmise that she slipped on it. I called an ambulance. I'm going to stay at the hospital with her. I know you need to be there with Daniel, and what did he eat by the way?"

"He needed to go to the library to work on a project with his friend and I gave him some money to eat out. Don't worry about Daniel he is fine. You just stay there with Naomi, and I hope she's going to be alright."

"Me too." My wife said in a distraught voice. I knew this was very painful for her because she loved her niece.

We ended the call, and I just sat there wondering how all of this happened. One moment we were having a disagreement and the next she was lying on the floor. My thoughts were interrupted when the doorbell rang. I trotted downstairs and answered the door and I was surprised to see Jermaine standing there.

"What are you doing here, man?"

Jermaine looked momentarily confused. "Remember I told you I would be stopping by today."

"Oh that." I said slapping my forehead. That was the last thing on my mind.

"Are you okay?" Jermaine asked giving me a peculiar look.

"It's been a long day, come in." I said stepping aside to let him in.

We walked to the living room and sat down. "So, what do you have to tell me?" I asked in a distracted tone.

"I thought about it, and I won't spy on Michelle. I really like her, and I can't do that to her. She just came over the ordeal with her surgery. So, if you want to give that recording to the police then go right ahead." Jermaine said seriously.

"Okay, you don't have to do it if you don't want to." I said. I had more important things on my plate than worrying about him spying on Michelle.

Jermaine looked at me like I had two heads. "Does that mean you're not going to the police?"

"No, I'm not going to the police. Now can you please leave my house." I was done talking to Jermaine.

"Thanks man. I don't know why you had a sudden change of heart, but I appreciate it." he said and got up from the couch. "I'll see you later." He said and left.

I was about to head back upstairs when Daniel walked in. "Hey dad."

"Hey, son."

"Is mom home?"

"No, she's at the hospital with Naomi. She took a fall at her apartment."

"Oh my God, is she okay?"

"Hopefully, so. Your mom probably will call soon to let us know something."

"We should go to the hospital to visit her."

"No, I don't think we should do that. She probably can't have many visitors and you have to go to school in the morning, so you can't be at the hospital all night."

"Okay, but let me know when mom calls." He said and then went upstairs.

I sat on the couch a ball of nerves. The hospital is the last place I wanted to be. If Naomi was finally talking there was no telling what she might say because she already was threatening to let the cat out of the bag. I was under so much stress and my head was pounding violently. My cell phone rang, and I quickly picked it up and answered it.

"It's worse than I thought." Valerie said and let out a soft cry. "When Naomi fell, she broke her neck. She is now paralyzed from the neck down, and she suffered a head injury that took away her ability to speak. It's just horrible." Valerie said and began sobbing.

A huge lump formed in my throat. "I'm so sorry babe." I managed to choke out.

"The police were on the scene, they are going to investigate, but to them they say it look like a freak accident."

At her talk of the police made me freeze up. What if one of her neighbors saw me or heard us arguing. We were pretty loud, but I couldn't come forward because coming forward would mean breaking my wife's heart.

"I'm going to bring Desmond home with me. He will have to live with us now." She said.

It was bitter sweet. I would finally have my son with me, but I didn't want to have him with me under these circumstances.

CHAPTER 19

Michelle

It was a week after Naomi's accident and her condition was still critical. I was feeling much better after my surgery and hadn't had any more headaches. I was missing a small patch of my hair on the side when they shaved it for the surgery, but I was able to cover it well with my hair. I was at the hospital along with Regina and Valerie. All three of were standing over Naomi's hospital bed. We had just finished praying for her. She had underwent two surgeries last week, and we were praying for a miracle. It was just horrible, such a beautiful young girl trapped inside her body. She couldn't speak or move at all. The doctor's explained that the damage to the part of her brain that controlled her speech was irreversible. They say she was suffering from aphasia. After praying for her we left her room because she could only have one visitor at a time. The doctor made a special exception for us because we wanted to pray for her.

"This is all too much, and she has insurance but it's not enough to cover everything, so I'm going to take on her medical bills." Valerie said.

I felt sympathy for her because she was a wreck. "Don't worry about the hospital bills. I don't mind helping out if you need me to."

"Oh no, I can't ask you to do that." Valerie said

"You didn't have to ask, I'm volunteering."

"I'm going to miss Naomi at the daycare. She was such a good worker." Regina said.

"Thank you both so much for coming here and praying for Naomi. I'm going to go home now. Jeff is home with Desmond, and I know he can use my help with him." She said and laughed softly. I gave Valerie a tight hug before she left.

"Poor thing." Regina said as she watched Valerie until she disappeared down the hallway. "But at least she can still see and talk to her niece. I would give anything to see and talk to my son one last time. I have an interview with the local TV station in a couple of hours. They are coming to my house and I want you to be there with me when I do it."

I stiffened. "Regina, you should give the interview because the focus should be on you as his mother.

"No." Regina said shaking her head. "My son deserves justice and if I have you a well -known Pastor, the daughter of the great Louis Davis asking for justice for my son, we can get the police department to search harder and maybe it can gain national exposure, and you can help me bring the focus on how Bradley was a good kid because they are highlighting the trouble he got into in the past."

That was the last thing I wanted. Because if it became a national case than sooner or later, they would find the trail that would lead to my daughter, but I couldn't deny her. "Okay." I reluctantly agreed.

Regina studied me for a moment. "You don't seem as if you really want to do this."

"Oh, it's not that. I just don't want to take the focus off you and Bradley."

"Don't worry about that. I need your support."

"And you will have it."

"Great." She said.

We left the hospital and went to Regina's house. I helped her pick out a nice outfit to wear on camera. I was already dressed nicely in a blouse and skirt. Finally, the news crew arrived, and we were seated comfortably on Regina's burgundy suede couch.

"Are you guys ready?" The young blond white woman asked us. We nodded yes, and she began the interview. "Hello, this is Melanie Dunn from channel thirteen news and I'm here with Regina Tyson and Pastor Michelle Roberts from God's Kingdom Worship Center right here in Kansas City and Faith and Love Christian Center in Memphis. They are here today to discuss the investigation into the death of Regina's son Bradley who was killed about a month and a half ago, and his killer is still at large." She then turned her attention to Regina. "What is it you would like to say today Miss Tyson?"

"It's been a nightmare living without my son. He has been in trouble in the past, but he was a very good young man that was on the right path. I want the police to try harder to bring his killer to justice."

"Yes, I can only imagine how dreadful this must be for you." Then she looked at me. "What would you like to add Pastor Roberts.

My stomach started twisting in knots, but it was important that I stayed calm. *You can do this?* I coached myself inwardly. "Bradley was a nice young man and a member of my church. Like Regina said Bradley had some troubles in the past, but that's not uncommon for teenage boys. And I know with a case like this that you have to bring up his past, but I think the focal point should be more on how his life had changed. It's important that Bradley gets justice, and I think any parent out there can agree with that."

"Very nicely said and I agree wholeheartedly with you. If anyone has any information that could lead to Bradley's killer, please call the number at the bottom of the screen." She ended the interview and shook our hands. "Thank you so much, and I hope and pray that the person who did this to Bradley will be caught soon." Melanie said and shook our hands.

After she left along with her camera crew, Regina turned towards me with tears in her eyes. "Thank you so much for doing this for me. I know that interview will have an impact on so many people."

"No, problem. That's what's friends are for." I said feeling like a wolf in sheep's clothing.

CHAPTER 20

Jeffrey

A couple of weeks passed by and I was feeling drained. Having Desmond around full-time was a lot of work. I hadn't taken care of a three-year old since Omar and Daniel were small. I was enjoying having him around though and so was Daniel and Valerie. Omar said he was going to spend the weekend with us when we told him that Desmond was living with us now. Naomi's hospital bills were a lot, and it was going to do major damage to our savings even though I had the money my father left me. Valerie told me Michelle had offered to help and as much as I didn't want to take her help, I knew we needed to. Valerie said she wanted to move Naomi home with us when she was released from the hospital, but I told her we should put her in a health care facility because they could take care of her better. Valerie pointed out that it would be more money, but it would be money well spent because I didn't think I could see Naomi everyday in my home in that condition.

I was in my office going over the letter all the deacon's got for the deacon's meeting we would be having next week. Pastor Dan would be hosting the meeting because Michelle had to head back to her church in Memphis next week. I had just finished reading my letter when there was a knock on my door. "Come in." I said. Tyler walked through the door shocking me.

"What are you doing, here?" I asked him.

Tyler shut the door behind him and walked in and sat down in the chair across from me, like he had an appointment or that it was perfectly normal for him to be in my office.

"I'm here on the behalf of Naomi because I love her, and we could have had an amazing future together."

"Is that right?" I asked trying to play it cool, but on the inside, I was sweating.

"Yes, I know it was you that caused her accident. Naomi is a beautiful young woman that had a bright future until you came in and messed that up. She was thinking about going to college to be a pediatric nurse because she loves children, but now she can't do any of it, and you should suffer the consequences."

"You don't know what you're talking about." I shot back.

"Actually, I do. I know you are the father of Naomi's baby, and I can lead the cops right to you. It won't be hard for me to convince them that you pushed her down."

"You wouldn't." I said trying to stop myself from jumping across the table and strangling him.

"Oh yes I would, Deacon. See that's why church people sicken me. You have a powerful position but you're a hypocrite. If your church knew what you were really all about, what would they think?" Tyler said with a scowl. When I didn't respond he continued speaking. "I'll tell you what, I won't tell the church or lead the police to you if you pay me."

"You've got to be kidding me? You're trying to blackmail me now?" I asked not believing his audacity.

Tyler snickered. "Write me a check for five thousand dollars and all your secrets are safe."

I was so mad I was afraid that if I opened my mouth fire would come out of it. There was nothing I could do, Tyler had me. I could call his bluff, but I didn't want to take that risk. "Fine." I said and unlocked my drawer and pulled out my checkbook and wrote him a check for five thousand dollars. I grudgingly slid the check to him. And he greedily picked it up and put it in his pocket. "You claim you love Naomi, but you're getting five thousand dollars out of it." I said angrily.

"I do love her. You're the one that doesn't care about her leaving her in the house helpless. She could have died if no one came there." He stood up.

"Now that you have my money you better not say a word." I said coldly. If Tyler crossed me there was no telling what I would do.

Tyler smirked. "Don't worry old man, your secrets are safe with me." He said and walked out the door and closed it behind him.

After he left, I took my arm and sent everything on my desk crashing to the floor. I was beyond angry. He just weaseled five thousand dollars out of me, after I had so many new bills to consider. But as mad as I was, I knew that I was reaping what I'd sown, and I wonder if my harvest was finished yet.

CHAPTER 21

Jeffrey

It was Saturday evening and me and Valerie were snuggled on the couch watching a movie. Daniel was out with his friends and Omar took Desmond to the mall with him. Omar had arrived home yesterday and would be returning to college tomorrow. I was happy to spend some alone time with my wife. With everything that happened we didn't have much time for romance anymore. Valerie had been so stressed, and I was delighted that she was relaxed comfortably in my arms. We were half way through the movie when movie when Omar walked in with Desmond. Desmond was eating a chocolate chip cookie.

"Hey guys." I greeted them.

"Did you have fun at the mall?" Valerie asked

"Yes, and he insisted on getting cookies before we left." Omar said to Valerie, but he was staring directly at me and I wondered why he was looking at me like that.

"That's nice. I'm glad you two had fun." Valerie said.

"Come on let's go upstairs." Omar said and led Desmond upstairs.

Omar returned downstairs about five minutes later. He sat down in the single chair beside us. "Dad, it's time you tell mom the truth or I will."

Valerie and I immediately pulled apart and sat up straight on the couch. "Omar, what are you talking about?" I asked him in a pleading voice.

"What's going on?" Valerie asked.

"Tell her Dad." Omar demanded giving me the look of death.

I just sat there frozen. *Was my son about to rat me out, and just how much did he know?*

When I remained silent, Omar began speaking. "Yesterday I took Desmond to get a DNA test. I have a friend there who is a nurse. I took the bottle of water you drunk out of the trashcan to use. I did take him to the mall, but we went to the hospital first. I got the results back today, and Desmond is your son."

Valerie gasped.

My heart was racing so fast and I started to perspire.

"When I caught you kissing Naomi a few years ago you swore it was a one-time thing, but after Naomi's accident, and Desmond coming to live with us something just didn't seem right. I didn't want you to make a fool out of my mother, so I had to know once and for all if Desmond was my brother and since Desmond is living here permanently his true paternity needs to be revealed."

I spent all this time trying to cover up my tracks and being blackmailed only to have my first-born son to come in here and blow up my spot. I jumped up off the couch and stood in front of Omar. "You ungrateful troublemaker, how dare you hit your mother with this!" I yelled in his face. I was about to pull him out of the chair when Valerie hopped up off the couch and ran upstairs. "I'm going to go check on your mother, and you better hope she forgives me or you're going to have to answer to me." I threatened. Omar didn't even flinch at my words.

I turned around and sprinted upstairs after Valerie. She was in our walk-in closet throwing all my clothes on the bed like a mad woman.

"Baby please stop it and listen to me for a moment."

Valerie threw a couple of my jeans on the bed and then looked at me. And the way she looked made me take a step back. She looked scarier than Sissy Spacek in the movie Carrie after she got the hog's blood thrown on her.

"Listen, I'm sorry about this." I said carefully

"You actually slept with my niece and got her pregnant, and then acted like Desmond was just your nephew." Valerie said in a faraway voice.

"I didn't want to hurt you."

"You were still sleeping with her weren't you." I just stared at her pleading with my eyes. My silence was all she needed to know I was guilty. My wife began attacking me like a mad woman.

I wrapped my arms tightly around her to block her blows. "Calm down and let me explain." I could feel Valerie's body trembling in my arms. I gently sat her down on the bed, and I sat next to her.

Valerie wiped her tears away with the back of her hand. "How could you take advantage of my niece like that? She was just a child."

"I was stupid, baby. I love you and our family."

Valerie shook her head. "I don't believe anything that comes out of your mouth. You were perfectly content on letting Desmond live here without telling me he was your son."

She had me there because I don't think I would ever tell her the truth on my own. I took her hand. "There is probably nothing I can say to make this right, but just please give me a chance to fix this."

"Don't listen to any of his crap mom."

I turned around and saw Omar standing in the doorway.

"Get out of here. This is between me and your mother."

Valerie pulled her hand away from mine. "He doesn't have to leave. He cared enough to tell me the truth. Valerie stood up and went back to the closet and start pulling my clothes out of the closet again.

I looked at Omar. "Are you happy now?"

"Actually, I am, but I will be happier when you leave this house."

"I'm not going anywhere." I said standing up.

"Yes, you are, please leave now." Valerie said.

"Where am I supposed to go?"

"I really don't care. Just leave, now." She ordered putting emphasis on the word now.

I looked back and forth at the angry faces of my wife and son and I knew I better get out of here fast before things got ugly. I got my suitcase out of the closet and put the clothes in it that Valerie had laid on the bed. Once I was done, I reached out to embrace Valerie, but she ducked out of the way. There was nothing else to be said, I walked towards the door and Omar moved aside to let me pass by and looked at me like I was the scum of the earth.

I went downstairs and out the door and put my suitcase in the car and got inside. I sat there for a moment thinking about everything that just happened. I put my face in my hands and shook my head miserably. My world had officially fell apart and I didn't know how I would put the pieces back together again.

CHAPTER 22

Michelle

Jermaine and I were sitting at my kitchen table enjoying Chinese take-out. We had been spending a lot of time together over the last couple of weeks. The church knew that we were dating, and they were supportive of our relationship. I felt so comfortable with him, and I could obviously trust him because I trusted him with my secret. Jeff had been in a downward spiral since Valerie kicked him out of the house. He was staying at a hotel, but my mother felt sorry for him and let him live with her. I couldn't believe that Jeff had been sleeping with Valerie's niece right under her nose and had a child by her. Jeff was real a piece of work. Hopefully now he would turn his life around. He hadn't been to church as much since his fall out with Valerie, and he hadn't been hassling me anymore. I guess his life was shaken up now, and he didn't have time to concern himself with me. I told my mother that given the situation that I may have to ask Jeff to step down as a deacon, but my mother told me to reconsider that, and I told her I would for now.

"I never get tired of eating sweet and sour chicken." Jermaine said.

"It's good, but I love the orange chicken." I said and then took a big bite of it.

Jermaine and I talked about our plans for next weekend and then my doorbell rang. "I'll be right back." I said and left the kitchen to answer the door. I was shocked to see Jason standing there and he didn't look happy. "What are you doing here?" I asked him.

"I'm here about our daughter. Can you please let me in?"

"Sure." I said and stepped aside to let him enter. I closed the door behind him, and we walked into the living room. "Now what's going on, and where is Courtney?"

"Courtney is at the detention center." He said staring a hole through me.

I felt like I was about to faint, so I sat on the couch and he sat next to me. "Say that again because I don't think I heard you right?"

Jason was about to respond, when Jermaine walked into the living room. "Is everything okay in here?" he asked noticing the tension between us.

"Jermaine this is…"

"Jason Roberts." He finished for him. "Of course, I know who he is. Nice to meet you." He said.

"Likewise, but if you don't mind, I need to speak to Michelle alone." Jason said firmly.

Jermaine looked at me as if the ask "What is going on?"

"It's okay Jermaine. I'll call you later." Jermaine looked disappointed but nodded in understanding and then left.

"Now are you going to stop this charade you're playing. I know you lied to the police about Courtney's whereabouts the night Bradley died, and you convinced her to do the same. You see Courtney started having nightmares. And finally, after having a terrible nightmare she broke down and told me what really happened with Bradley. Keeping a secret like that was slowly killing her, so I booked the first flight here, and we then we went to the police department where she told them everything."

"You should have let me know you were going to do that." I said in a trembling voice. He had pulled the rug out from underneath me.

"Why should I when all you were going to do is tell her to keep her mouth shut not caring what it was doing to her. That's right she told me that's what you would always say when she mentioned revealing the truth."

Now I was becoming angry. "How dare you say that to me. I love my daughter and care about her. That's why I lied to the police because I didn't want her to be labeled as a murderer."

Jason shook his head. "She is not a murderer. It was an accident, and you should have reminded her of that, but instead you told her to lie because you were trying to protect your position at the church. You didn't want to deal with the blowback. After your recent health scare, I'm surprised that you didn't come forward with the truth."

I flinched at his words because they were true. I was worried about my position at the church. He was right I should have come forward after having successful brain surgery. Him and Courtney had been so happy that everything went okay with my surgery. "I love my daughter and have her best interest at heart."

"Of course, you love her, but I think your position at the church mattered to you more than what holding all this in was doing to her, and it was your best friend's son. I don't understand how you could comfort Regina and give interviews asking for justice." He said shaking his head. "That's why our marriage didn't work because you were more concerned about yourself then our marriage."

"You can't blame our failed marriage on me because you were so wrapped up in your career and kissing another woman." I said angrily.

"I loved you more than anything, but I knew I would never come first for you and neither does our daughter. I'm letting you know all this because it will be hitting the news soon, and we need to go see Courtney. It was clearly an accident, but since she got rid of the murder weapon and her clothes on the night of the incident, it's going to be a little harder to prove. But they are going to go back over the evidence."

I sat there for a moment knowing that life as me and Courtney knew it would be over, and I was overcome with emotion and began sobbing.

Jason put his arm around me and pulled me to his chest. "It's going to be okay, we are going to make sure of that." He said. But I wasn't sure if I believed him.

We took a moment to gather ourselves and then we headed to the detention center to see Courtney. Once we checked in the officer led us to the visiting area. Courtney came out a few minutes later, and when I saw her, I almost burst into tears she looked so frighten and lost. Courtney was just sixteen years old, she should be worried about going to the prom and looking forward to graduating not worrying about fighting off a murder charge.

She sat down in front of us. "Mom I'm so sorry I couldn't hold it in anymore she said miserably."

"No, you have nothing to apologize for. I owe you an apology. I should have never lied to the police and asked you to go along with it. But don't worry sweetie your dad and I are here for you, and you will beat this."

A glimmer of hope flashed in Courtney's eyes. "I want to get out of here. I hate it in here." she wailed.

Jason reached across the table and grabbed Courtney's hands. "I know it's hard, but you have to stay strong. We're going to get you a good lawyer and you will get off."

"But do I really deserve to get off?" Courtney asked softly.

"Of course, you deserve to get out of here. It was just an accident." I said feeling my heart break. Seeing her in here was just too much for me.

We sat with Courtney for about an hour trying to lift her spirits, but it didn't seem to do much good because she still seemed to be in a gloomy mood. And who could blame her. I hated to admit it, but things didn't look too good for her.

When Jason and I left the detention center, I felt defeated. The drive to my house was quiet. The trouble Courtney was in was weighing heavily on both of us. As soon as I turned the corner to my home, I spotted three news vans and I sighed heavily. This was the last thing that I needed. Jason parked the car while the news crew stared at us, anxiously waiting for us to get out of the car.

"I'll be right by your side. Just ignore their questions." He couched me. I just sat there stubbornly. "Come on Michelle, you can't sit in here forever."

He was right. I took a deep breath and we both exited the car and I was met with question after question. "Pastor Roberts why did you lie for your daughter? Was it really an accident? Will you be resigning as Pastor?" I ignored all their questions as Jason shielded me. We finally made it to the door, and I hurried to unlock it and Jason, and I quickly went inside.

"Wow, this is what I have to look forward to for a while." I said as I walked into the living room and plopped down on the couch.

Jason sat beside me. "That makes the both of us. I'm sure people will have plenty of questions for me especially when I get back to L.A., but what you should do is to put out a public statement. Maybe a statement from both of us." Jason suggested.

"I'm not ready to talk to anyone." I was about to say something else when my house phone and cell phone started ringing and Jason's cell phone rang as well. We just looked at each other.

"You see what I mean. We need to say something and quick." Jason advised.

"You're right, but I don't know what to say."

"Me either, but I'm sure we will think of something." Jason said.

No matter what we said I knew that things would never be the same.

CHAPTER 23

Jeffrey

I was sitting on the couch watching the news. To say I was depressed would be an understatement. I had been basically glued to the couch. I only left to eat, sleep, shower. I haven't even been really handling my business at church. No one knew that Desmond was my son yet, but I know it was just a matter of time. My mother was trying to be patient with me, but she was growing tired of my behavior. She basically told me to get off my behind and get my family back. I had called Valerie repeatedly trying to apologize but she would not answer any of my calls. Of course, Omar wasn't talking to me. He was so much like me. Daniel came by to see me. He didn't understand how I could do something like this. I apologized to him, and it seems like he was trying to forgive me. I knew it was going to be a long road to get my family back, but I wasn't giving up.

I was snapped out of my thoughts when I heard the next headline. "Breaking news, Courtney Roberts, the daughter of prominent pastor Michelle Roberts and famous gospel singer Jason Roberts has just confessed to accidently shooting nineteen-year old Bradley Tyson. Bradley Tyson was a teen from Kansas City, Missouri who was killed about two months ago, his murder was unsolved until now. Apparently, Courtney and Jason had been dating. Pastor Michelle Roberts told authorities that her daughter was with her at the time of Bradley Tyson's murder, but we now know that isn't true. Pastor Roberts recently gave an interview asking for justice for Bradley. This is an ironic turn of events. I don't have all the details, but I will keep you updated as they become available." The reporter said

"Say it isn't so." My mother said.

I turned around and saw the shocked look on her face and I was shocked as well. I knew Michelle was hiding something, but I didn't think it was anything like this. I knew things were about to get very bad for Michelle, and this is what I wanted, to see her fall, but now that the moment was finally here, I took no pleasure in it. My life was in shambles and now I could relate to what she was going through. I felt bad for my niece Courtney.

"It's a shame that they never discussed Bradley's death on CNN, but the moment his death is connected to Courtney it gets national attention because she comes from a prominent family." My mother said in disgust.

"I can't even imagine what Courtney's been going through." I said.

"Both you and Michelle are going through something and it's time this family pull together because it's the only way we will get through this. "I'm going to call Michelle now, to see what's going on and exactly what her part in all of this is." My mother said and left the room.

I let my mother's words sink in. We did need to pull together in our time of need, but I don't know how much help I could be right now because I was so lost without my family.

CHAPTER 24

Michelle

The next few weeks were a whirlwind for me. Considering everything that happened I stepped down as Pastor and let Pastor Dan to take over. My church family didn't ask me to, but I felt it was best because I knew they couldn't fully trust me right now, and I didn't need to be up there preaching when my congregation didn't know how to feel about me now. I called my assistant pastor in Memphis and told him what was going on. He said that the media had been by the church too, and he didn't know what to tell them. I felt horrible about the awful position I had put everyone in, and the media was even saying that I was not living up to my father's legacy and I would probably destroy it. A lot of talk shows were talking about the scandal and asked me if me and my daughter would like to come on their show to explain what really happened. I declined all the invitations. Jason was going through the same thing, but most of the attention was focused on me. Jason and I released a statement saying that I take full responsibility for my part in this and we asked for privacy for our family. It helped calm down the press some. The talk shows wouldn't let up though. They still asked for me to come on their show, but I didn't want to go through that, and I didn't want to put Courtney through it either. She was extremely depressed and had lost weight. Jason and I tried to cheer her up as much as we could when we visited her. That hurt me terribly because I knew how disappointed my father would be in me. But I had to stay focused on Courtney's case, so I hired a lawyer to help out Courtney, and he said it was a good chance that the case would be dropped but what was giving them pause is the fact that she didn't just call the cops after it happened and tell them exactly what happened, and I told him them it was my fault, that Courtney wanted to tell the truth, but I convinced her not to. But he said it was still Courtney's decision to run away and throw away evidence. Jason was right by my side through all of this and we both fasted during the whole ordeal. Leslie sent her support, but she let Jason and I handle it as a family. Jermaine was offering his support and was giving me a shoulder to lean on as well. The media had been all over me. They showed up at my house and even came by the church, but Pastor Dan and the deacons did a good job at keeping them at bay. I understood why everyone wanted answers. I was a Pastor so how could I lie to the police and try to cover up what my daughter did?

Courtney's lawyer told me not to talk to Regina during all of this because it could look bad in Courtney's defense, but I disobeyed him, and I called her, but she didn't answer my calls and she didn't answer the door when I went over. I felt I owed her an apology and to tell her why I convinced Courtney to do this. But it didn't take long for Regina and her mother to publicly show their outrage. Regina had given interviews saying that she couldn't believe that I preached at her son's funeral and let her cry on my shoulder without telling her that my daughter was responsible. Her interviews were making it harder for me, but I deserved it.

I was on my way over to my mother's house because she wanted to talk to me about everything that had been going on. I had talked to her once and explained everything in detail about what happened. My mother was understandably upset with me and she blamed me for what Courtney now had to go through. My feelings were hurt after she said that to me, so I stopped taking her calls. I had enough on my plate, and I needed only positivity around me, but my mother said it was important that I come by the house today, so I decided I would.

When I arrived at my mother's house, I parked my car and walked to the door and knocked.

My mother answered the door with a serious look on her face. "Why don't you come in dear." She said and stepped aside to let me in. Once I had entered, she closed the door behind me, and she told me to come sit in the den.

Once we arrived in the den, I saw Jeff sitting on the couch and I turned around to leave but my mother stopped me by grabbing my arm. "No, you don't, we are going to sit down as a family."

I reluctantly turned around and sat on the couch across from Jeff but instead of the usual arrogant look on his face he had a contrite look. This surprised me, but I wasn't going to let my guard down. My mother sat down on the single chair between Jeff and me.

"Michelle when you returned to Kansas City to head Louis's church, I was ecstatic. My husband was gone but my daughter was returning home and to me that was the bright spot in this tragedy. My family was finally back together, and I was hoping things would go well." She stopped talking and turned her attention to Jeff. "But Jeff you couldn't let go of the fact that your father left the church to Michelle instead of you, and you went out of your way to make her feel uncomfortable and unwelcomed. You were her older brother and you should have been more supportive. Because of all the tension I couldn't even get my family together for a simple Sunday dinner." My mother then turned her attention to me. "I know your reason for lying to the police was so you could protect Courtney, but if Jeff hadn't been waiting on you to

fall, I believed there is a chance you wouldn't have done this."
Tears started falling down my mother's face.

"Mom, I'm so sorry, and you're right I should have supported
my sister." I was so busy waiting for her downfall that I didn't
stop to think what this was doing to you." Jeff said with a
despondent look on his face.

This scene was causing me to tear up because there was so
much truth in my mother's words. I went over to my mother and
hugged her tightly. Her body shook in my arms. Jeff and I had
been so selfish thinking about ourselves that we didn't check on
mother like we should, and even though I hadn't been there for her
like I should she still was there for me after my surgery. "I'm
sorry and I promise to do better." I whispered in her ear. We cried
together for about five minutes and then we pulled apart and I sat
back down on the couch.

"Michelle, I'm so sorry. I was waiting to see you fall when it
was my life that could blow up at any second. What I done could
cause a huge scandal to the church if it gets out. I'm so ashamed
of myself. I even sent in Jermaine to get close to you by
blackmailing him, so he could find dirt on you. He agreed to do it,
but he refused to tell me anything about you. Bottom line is I was
always jealous of you because you are what I wished I could be.
You are so much like Dad."

I stared at my brother in shock. I wasn't shocked about him
being jealous of me because I always knew that. It was what he
just told me about Jermaine, I knew he had asked me out, out of
the blue, but I didn't question it. I wanted to believe that he really
liked me.

When Jeff saw the look on my face he tried to explain. "He agreed to do it because I didn't give him a choice, but I'm telling you he really likes you."

I shook my head in disbelief. I was starting to feel better about everything until this latest confession from my brother. I took a deep breath and reminded myself that we all had done some awful things. "I forgive you Jeff. Before all this came out, I was going to ask you to step down as a deacon, but I think that's between you and God. You can choose how you want to handle this because honestly, I don't think the church can handle anymore bad news about their leaders.

My mother smiled. "Now that's what I liked to hear. It's time that we all start acting like family again. It's what your father would have wanted.

I agreed with my mother, but after everything that happened, I needed to figure out what I truly wanted and what was best for me and my family.

CHAPTER 25

Jeffrey

After finally making amends with my sister, I figured it was time to get my family back. So, about a week later, on a Saturday, I headed back to my house. I walked up to the door and was surprised when my key still worked. Once inside I walked into the living room. I knew Valerie wasn't home because her car wasn't there, and Daniel was most likely out with his friends. I stood there for a moment looking around and at that moment I realized home much I missed being home with my family. I didn't know what to say to Valerie or where to begin, but all I could do is apologize again and say what was in my heart. I had been praying all week. I was prepared to do whatever I could to get my family back.

I went upstairs to my bedroom and laid on the bed. How I missed sleeping next to my wife. I laid there thinking about how I could be so stupid in the first place. I don't know how long I laid there thinking, but I was snapped out of my thoughts when Valerie walked into the bedroom with Desmond right behind her.

Valerie had a tired and weary look on her face. "Jeff, why are you in my room laying on my bed?" Valerie asked in an exasperated voice.

I noticed how she put the emphasis on the word my. "It's my bedroom too, so I can lay on the bed if I want to." I said with a smile. But Valerie didn't smile back.

Desmond walked over to me. "Hey Uncle Jeff."

"Hey little man." I said

"Desmond why don't you come downstairs to the kitchen with me, so I can fix you a snack." Valerie suggested. Desmond cheerfully agreed to go downstairs with her and get a snack. Valerie gave me a sharp look before taking Desmond out of the room.

I sat up on the bed. "At least she didn't kick me out." I said to myself.

Valerie came back to the bedroom about fifteen minutes later. "Jeff you need to leave. I'm really not in the mood to deal with you right now." She said in a tired voice.

"What's wrong?" I asked her.

Valerie let out a tired sighed and sat on the edge of the bed. "I just got back from taking Desmond to the facility to see Naomi. It's so hard seeing her like that. Desmond talks to her, but he doesn't understand why she can't talk to him or pick him up. I feel bad about not bringing her here to live, but the facility is so much better for her. It's a nice setup there, and I won't be able to provide her with the care that she needs."

"I know how hard all this is for you, and it doesn't help that you have an idiot for a husband." I said setting the mood for the apology I was about to give her.

"You're right about that. You know Jeff I knew that you cheated on me when you left college." My eyes went wide. "Don't look so surprised. Of course, I knew. Women talk you know, but I loved you and I knew how hard it was for you after you failed college. But I never would have guessed that you would have started sleeping around with my niece, and then to get her pregnant." Valerie said and shook her head before continuing. "I feel so stupid because I never saw it, but I blame you and not her because she was a child dealing with the death of her mother."

"You're right it is my fault because I was the adult, and you should never feel stupid. You just had faith in your husband, and I let you down. I know saying sorry isn't going to be enough, but if you would give me a chance, I will be a better man for you." I pleaded

"I want to give us another try but there is so much to deal with. Desmond is now living here, but how should we tell him the truth that you are really his father, and I'm tired of seeing you go after your sister. My only sister and sibling is dead and I wish she were still here, and you have a great sister and you mistreat her. You must be happy at the latest news about her."

"No, I'm not. I had a long talk with Michelle and my mother. I apologized to them both. From here on out my sister has my support, and we will seek direction from God on when and how to tell Desmond that I'm his father. The church doesn't need to know I'm his father until we deal with this as a family."

Valerie's face softened, and I knew I was close to getting her back. "We can try, but this will take time. I'm glad you are supporting your sister because she's going to need it. Both of you haven't been back to church and it's not the same without her. There is constant chatter around the church. People are on the fence. They really don't know how to feel about the situation."

"I know, and it will help if I come back and speak some encouraging words to the congregation." I said.

Valerie smiled. "Now that's what I want to see you supporting your sister."

Valerie and I had a long talk, but I didn't tell her about my part in what happened to Naomi. It was an accident and I felt like telling her what really happened wouldn't do any good at this point. After we finished our talk, we had dinner as a family. Daniel was happy to have me back home, but I knew getting back into Omar's good graces would be a lot of hard work, but I was up for the challenge.

CHAPTER 26

Michelle

The day had finally arrived, Jason and I sat nervously in the courtroom waiting to hear Courtney's fate. The judge just got finished listening to evidence from both sides, and now she was going to decide if the charges against Courtney will be dropped or if the manslaughter charge would stick.

"After reviewing evidence from both sides, I have concluded that the charges against Courtney Roberts will be dropped, but she will have to serve community service for destroying evidence. I'll set a later date to discuss how much community service she will have to serve."

Tears of joy streamed down my face, and Jason squeezed my hand. Courtney turned around and gave us a small smile. Tears were running down her face as well. She would have to serve community service, but that was a small price to pay. I looked on the other side of the courtroom at Regina and her mother. They both were holding each other and sobbing. I watched them feeling momentarily sad for them. They let go of each other and Regina and I looked at each other. Her expression was pained, and I hoped my expression was saying how sorry I was for all of this. My attention was pulled away when everyone started leaving and Courtney hugged me and Jason.

"See sweetie, I told you everything will be fine." I said.

Her lawyer who was a handsome black man in his late twenties stood there and watched the moment between us before interrupting. "We just have to get Courtney processed out and then she will be ready to go in about twenty minutes."

"Okay, and thanks for everything." I said, and Jason thanked him too.

"No problem." He said and led Courtney out of the courtroom.

Regina and her mother stood there staring at us. I went over to them. "Regina I'm sorry for everything and I would like us to talk about everything that happened." I said humbly.

"Get away from us, Michelle. You have nothing to say to my daughter. You're not a real friend. You had plenty of time to tell her everything, but you were too busy showing fake concern in interviews. You are nothing like your father and he is probably rolling over in his grave at your behavior. To think that I was so grateful you were back in Kansas City, but you being here caused all this pain." She shouted angrily.

"Don't bring my father into this." I said boiling on the inside. I could admit I was wrong, but my father should be left out of this. Jason can behind me and put his hands on my shoulders

"Stop it you two. This is not helping, and I agree. Michelle we do need to talk. Just call me and let me know when." Regina said and guided her angry mother out of the courtroom.

"Don't let people get to you. You know they are going to try to compare you to your father after all of this." Jason said.

"I know. I'm not going to focus on that. Our daughter is coming home." I said

About thirty minutes later Courtney was released and Jason and I happily took her home. Once home Courtney jumped in the shower and said she wanted to order pizza and wings. We happy obliged her and we all sat around and ate. Courtney was in good spirits, but I knew that this situation would still weigh on her, but Jason and I would support her in whatever way we could.

We enjoyed the rest of our evening and the next day I went to Regina's place to talk. Regina answered the door with a stiff smile on her face.

"Hello Regina." I spoke awkwardly.

"Come in." She simply said and stepped aside so I could enter. Once inside we went into the living room and sat down on her couch to talk. "Can I get you anything to drink or anything?" Regina asked.

"No, I want to apologize for keeping the truth from you." I said. I wanted to go ahead and get it out.

"That's what I don't understand why you felt the need to lie."

"I was scared for Courtney's future and I was worried if there would be any blowback on the church." I admitted.

Regina shook her head. "I just can't believe you've been by my side while I cried and asked for justice for Bradley's killer. You were my best friend and you didn't trust me with the truth."

"I know. I should have never lied to the police about Courtney's whereabouts. I'm so sorry."

"I'm sorry to, but I'm glad to know what finally happened to Bradley. Just so you know I don't blame Courtney, but I am bothered by the fact that she chose to run away instead of asking for help. I didn't even know that Bradley owned a gun."

"It's a devastating situation, and if you want, I can still be here for you."

Regina looked at me sadly. "It won't be the same. I don't know if I can fully trust you anymore."

Her words hurt me, but she was right. I know that things would never be the same between us. After she said that there was nothing left to be said and I apologized again before leaving. On my way home, I knew there was a lot more apologizing that I had to do.

CHAPTER 27

Michelle

The following Sunday I sat on the first pew with Courtney sitting beside me listening to Pastor Dan speak. Pastor Dan is a light brown man in his early fifties. "As you all know Pastor Roberts and her daughter Courtney are here. Today Pastor Roberts is going to talk to you about that situation and keep you heart and ears open while she speaks. Pastor Roberts please take the podium." Pastor Dan said

Courtney squeezed my hand to let me know I would be fine. I slowly stood up with my heart beating wildly in my chest. I walked to the podium and looked ahead at the congregation. The whole church was quiet waiting to hear my explanation. "Good morning everyone, I want to thank all of you for coming here this morning. When I came back here to lead this church, I wanted to make my father proud. That was my number one priority, but that was a mistake because pleasing God should be at the top of my list. Since I wasn't putting God first the moment a difficult situation arose, I chose to lie and keep a secret because I wanted to protect my daughter and I didn't want any shame to come to my father's church. And that one lie has broken my congregation's trust and ruined a longtime friendship I had. Even with a recent health scare I still didn't reveal the truth. I had a tumor removed from my brain a few weeks back." I saw the shocked looks on the congregation faces. I had chosen to not tell anyone besides family about my surgery because I didn't want the congregation and the public to worry about my condition. The last thing I needed was for everyone to think that I wasn't well enough to run the church. "I want to say to you all that I'm sorry that I didn't step up and do what God would want me to do in my moment of crisis. The sad thing about it is my father would have wanted me to tell the truth no matter what. I have failed you all, but hopefully you all will forgive me. I have decided to officially resign as the Pastor of this church." I saw shocked expressions on the congregation faces, but I continued speaking. "I have built my own church Faith and Love Christian Center and that's where God wants me to be. I know this was my father's wish, but I must be where God wants me to be. I can still come here and preach from time to time, but I will be returning to Memphis. Pastor Dan is more than qualified to lead the church. God bless you all." Everyone stood up and applauded and I gave the podium to Pastor Dan and returned to my seat.

Last night while praying, I heard it in my spirit that God wanted me to return to Memphis. I would have to talk to the judge to see if Courtney could do her community service in Memphis. It's probably what He was trying to tell me all along, but my judgement was clouded by my grief. I sat there listening as Pastor Dan preached. He did an excellent job. I know my father wanted me to be the leader, but Pastor Dan has been his right-hand man for years and deserved the job. Who knew if Jeff got his act together completely maybe he would be on his way to leading the church. And I felt like he was beginning to turn things around because he came to church with his wife and three sons, and they all looked happy. I really wished him well and I could see he was trying to be a better man. He even came by the house to check on Courtney after she was released. Our church was recorded and broadcast on BET and other networks so I was happy that the world would be able to see me apologize and accept responsibility for my actions.

After service ended, I headed home to my mother's house for Sunday dinner. Jeff and his family were there as well. We had a great time as a family, and my mother told me she was saddened that I was leaving Kansas City, but I had to return to the church that I had built. I had called my assistant pastor last night to tell him I was returning and he as delighted. I told him that I would explain and apologize to the church, but he said that they were on my side and passionately stood up for me to anyone who would try to bad mouth me and I was delighted to hear that.

After dinner I drove home, and Courtney went upstairs to her room. I was about to head upstairs and shower when my doorbell rang. I went to the door and answered it. Jermaine was standing there with a smile on his face. "Hey Michelle, can I come in and talk to you?" he asked

I smiled back and invited him inside. I hadn't talked to him much because I was so focused on Courtney's case. We sat on the couch.

"That was a nice speech you gave, but I have to say I'm a little disappointed to hear that you will be returning back to Memphis. Where does that leave us?"

"Jeff told me that he blackmailed you into asking me out and spying on me." Jermaine's mouth went wide. "But don't worry I don't blame you and I'm not mad at you. However, I don't think things are going to work out with us right now. You have an addiction that I don't think you've quite kicked yet, and you need to focus on your relationship with your ex-wife and daughter, and I need to focus on being there for Courtney and making sure she's alright."

A disappointed look came across Jermaine's face. "I really like you Michelle and I think we could have had something special despite how things started between us."

"I agree, but the timing isn't right. We have to get our houses in order before we can even think about getting involved."

"You're right." Jermaine reluctantly agreed.

"Who knows what the future will hold. If it's meant to be, we will find our way back to each other." I said.

Jermaine leaned forward and kissed me on the lips, his lips on mine felt so good and I deepened the kiss. I finally pulled away afraid things would go too far.

Jermaine cupped my face with his hand and stared lovingly into my eyes. "Good-bye for now, Michelle." He said and let my face go. He then left leaving me with a yearning feeling.

CHAPTER 28

Jeffrey

It is two years later, and my life is going well. I introduced Desmond as my son a year ago. The church was shocked, and Pastor Dan asked me to step down from being a Deacon for a while, and I agreed I should. He talked to me and Valerie and prayed for us, and I was glad that he was now the man in charge of my father's church. Stepping down caused me to be more focused on God's word. It was nice going to church with my family and listening to the word without all the extra responsibilities. I grew as a Christian and everyone could see it. Especially my mom, wife, and Michelle. My son Omar was harder to convince. He was so stubborn like me. Eventually he came around and our relationship is better. I'm sad to say that Naomi's condition hasn't improved. Pastor Dan reinstated me as a Deacon a few months ago and I was happy and proud, and I am really doing an amazing job as a Deacon. If my father was still alive, he would be so proud of me. I was finally the man he had always wanted me to be. That thought only made me hold stronger to God's word.

CHAPTER 29

Michelle

My life is back on track now and I feel blessed because I didn't know if it would ever be. Courtney is doing well, and she will be graduating in June. That fateful day still gets to her from time to time, but she knows she has a great support system. My relationship with Jeff had improved tremendously. We always had a good time together whenever I visited Kansas City. Regina and I were talking again, and I visited her sometimes when I was in Kansas City. She is still grieving Bradley's death, but she is doing much better now. Things between us are better, but it's not like it was before and I don't know if it will ever be. Jermaine moved to Memphis a year ago and joined my church. He said he had kicked his addiction and that his relationship with his ex-wife and daughter had improved. We are seeing each other again and Jermaine proposed to me yesterday. I accepted, and we are planning our wedding for next year. I met his daughter and she liked me a lot, I got along with his ex-wife as well. My family is happy for me, especially my mother who knew Jermaine was right for me all along. I didn't think my life would be this good again after the lie I told, but I owe it to God for His grace and mercy.

The Pastor's Lie Shanika Roach

Made in the USA
Middletown, DE
08 January 2021

31077536R00090